–The–
Runaway's
Revenge

Trailblazer Books

TITLE	HISTORIC CHARACTERS
Abandoned on the Wild Frontier	Peter Cartwright
Attack in the Rye Grass	Marcus & Narcissa Whitman
The Bandit of Ashley Downs	George Müller
The Betrayer's Fortune	Menno Simons
The Chimney Sweep's Ransom	John Wesley
Danger on the Flying Trapeze	Dwight L. Moody
Escape from the Slave Traders	David Livingstone
Flight of the Fugitives	Gladys Aylward
The Hidden Jewel	Amy Carmichael
Imprisoned in the Golden City	Adoniram and Ann Judson
Kidnapped by River Rats	William & Catherine Booth
Listen for the Whippoorwill	Harriet Tubman
The Queen's Smuggler	William Tyndale
Quest for the Lost Prince	Samuel Morris
The Runaway's Revenge	John Newton
Shanghaied to China	Hudson Taylor
Spy for the Night Riders	Martin Luther
The Thieves of Tyburn Square	Elizabeth Fry
Trial by Poison	Mary Slessor
The Warrior's Challenge	David Zeisberger

–The–
Runaway's
Revenge

Dave & Neta Jackson

Illustrated by Julian Jackson

BETHANY HOUSE PUBLISHERS
MINNEAPOLIS, MINNESOTA 55438

Inside illustrations by Julian Jackson.
Cover illustration by Catherine Reishus McLaughlin.

Published by Bethany House Publishers
A Ministry of Bethany Fellowship, Inc.
11300 Hampshire Ave. South
Minneapolis, Minnesota 55438

Printed in the United States of America

Library of Congress Cataloging-in-Publication Data

Jackson, Dave.
    The runaway's revenge / Dave and Neta Jackson ; text illustrations
by Julian Jackson.
       p.   cm. — (Trailblazer books ; #18)
    Summary: Thirteen-year-old Hamilton Jones seeks revenge against
the former captain of the ship on which his mother had been taken from
Africa to slavery in the Colonies.
    ISBN 1–55661–471–3
    1. Newton, John, 1725–1807—Juvenile fiction. [1. Newton, John,
1725–1807—Fiction. 2. Slave trade—Fiction. 3. Christian life—
Fiction.] I. Jackson, Neta. II. Jackson, Julian, ill. III. Title.
IV. Series.
PZ7.J132418Ru   1995
[Fic]—dc20   95–43622
                                                      CIP
                                                      AC

Though there is no record that John Newton was ever confronted by a slave or the descendant of a slave, all the other details of Newton's life are authentic.

Hamilton Jones and Benjamin T. Bowdoin and all the events related directly to them are fictional.

DAVE AND NETA JACKSON are a husband/wife writing team who have authored or coauthored many books on marriage and family, the church, and relationships, including the books accompanying the Secret Adventures video series, the Pet Parables series, and the Caring Parent series.

They have three children: Julian, the illustrator for the Trailblazer series, Rachel, a college student, and Samantha, their Cambodian foster daughter. They make their home in Evanston, Illinois, where they are active members of Reba Place Church.

CONTENTS

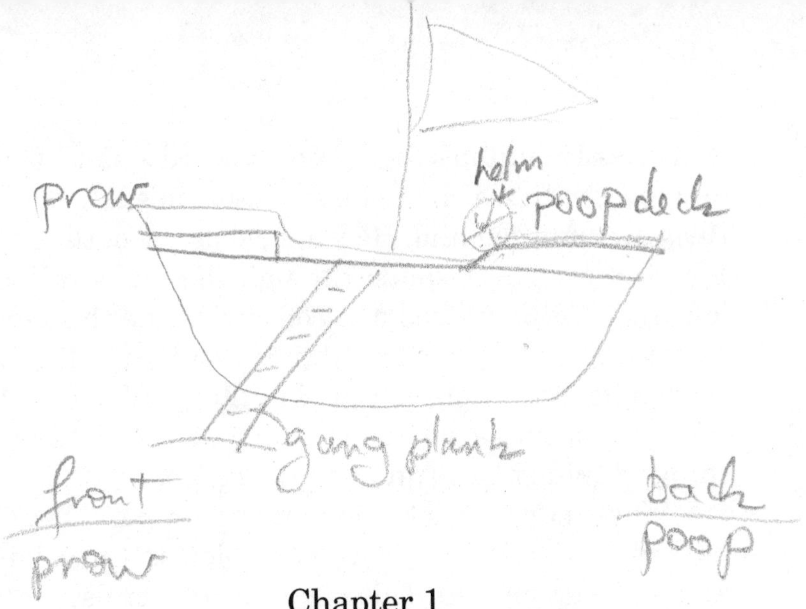
prow
helm
poop deck
gang plank
front
prow
back
poop

Chapter 1

The Vicious Triangle

In the early morning light, Hamilton Jones stood quietly on the deck behind his master, Benjamin T. Bowdoin. The old gentleman leaned against the damp railing as the outgoing tide swung the three-masted ship slowly around in the harbor of Charles Town in the Colony of South Carolina.

Back on the poop deck the pilot spoke to the captain, and the captain gave an order to the helmsman. He spun the wheel. There was a creaking in the rigging, and a sail caught the last of the night's offshore breeze and snapped tight.

The *Hawthorne* was underway!

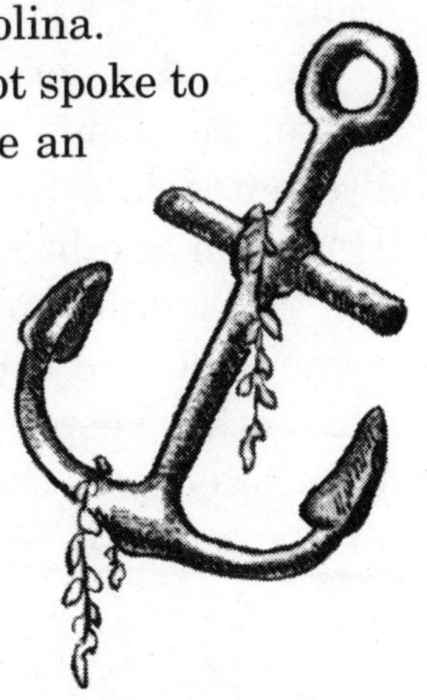

It was Hamilton's first time on board a ship. The quietness with which the huge vessel glided through the water amazed him. He watched as the outline of Fort Sullivan took shape through the mists to his left. In 1775 there was a lot of talk in the thirteen colonies about independence, and quiet Fort Sullivan was an important place. But Hamilton couldn't wait to see the open sea with its crashing waves. He knew things wouldn't be so quiet on the ocean.

"What do you think you're doing up here, boy?" barked Benjamin Bowdoin. "Get below to the cabin and make up my bed. This is no vacation cruise, you know. I'm on business."

"Yes, sir," mumbled Hamilton as he lowered his eyes. He was only thirteen, but he knew how a slave must act if he wanted to survive.

Mr. Bowdoin's cabin was not actually below the main deck but forward of the captain's cabin under the poop deck. Hamilton went there without complaint and made up his master's bed, arranging his personal things for him. The boy was not sure what to do next.

He had replaced Old George as Mr. Bowdoin's personal servant because Old George's failing health prevented him from making a long sea voyage. So Hamilton had been selected to accompany the master to England to sell his cotton. Most plantation owners worked through agents, but Bowdoin didn't trust other people where his fortune was concerned, especially when there was so much talk of revolution in the colonies. Bowdoin saw to business himself even though he, too, was old and in poor health.

As he worked in the small cabin, Hamilton counted himself lucky. The old man wanted him near at all times to serve his every need. Therefore, Hamilton had not been forced to bunk down in the hold with the cargo as would most blacks. Instead, Bowdoin had arranged for Hamilton to sleep in a small closet across the passage from his own cabin. It was dark and stuffy and the best he could do for a bed was a thickly folded piece of canvas on the floor, but it was his—his very own nook.

Hamilton finished in his master's cabin and tossed his own small sack of personal items into his nook. The ship was starting to move from side to side with the waves, and Hamilton was eager to go up and catch a look at the real sea, but he hesitated to face the old man again. Instead, he decided to explore the ship.

Along the passageway, he found some narrow steps and headed down. *Now I must be below deck,* thought Hamilton as he worked his way forward. He heard voices coming toward him and was about to turn back when he noticed another set of steps going even lower. He slipped farther down into the dark depths of the ship.

The boy felt his way along until a heavy door blocked the passage. He felt around and gave a tug on a large ring. The door opened. Far ahead, in what seemed to be a huge room, there hung a lantern, swinging slowly from side to side with the movement of the ship. He was in the ship's hold, and familiar smells told him that much of the cargo was cotton and tobacco.

But there was another smell, a foul smell as if someone had been sick or had even died. He moved cautiously forward, amazed at the huge timbers lacing the low ceiling. He stepped cautiously, listening to see if anyone else was there with him. He wasn't hurting anything, but few people would believe a black boy caught in a place he didn't belong.

The ship gently creaked and groaned, and a rat scared Hamilton as it scurried across his path, but soon he became certain that no one else was in the hold.

When he got to the lamp, he could see better. There was a small area without any cargo, and Hamilton moved toward the rounded sides of the ship. Into a beam above his head a row of spikes had been pounded. Curious, Hamilton moved closer, then froze in his tracks. From each spike hung a pair of leg-irons. Looking around, he saw that each beam was outfitted with the same hardware.

Hamilton felt a sudden stab of fear. Why would a ship need hundreds of leg-irons? And then the answer hit him. This was not a common merchant ship; it was a slave ship! The same kind that had brought his mother as a young girl from Africa!

Fear was replaced by a flash of anger. He had heard about slave traders. The ships that brought slaves to America from their homes in Africa were then filled with molasses from sugar cane, tobacco, and cotton—all raised by slave labor—bound for En-

gland. In England the ships were loaded with muskets, gunpowder, rum made from the molasses, and other consumer goods to be taken to Africa and traded for more slaves. It was a vicious triangle—one that had brought misery to his mother and death to his grandfather, a man Hamilton had never known.

In the dim light of the lantern, the boy cautiously stepped toward the racks that lined the hold. Now they were piled with bales of cotton and tobacco, but weeks or even days before they had been crammed with human cargo. Hamilton reached out and gingerly touched the shelf as though it were something holy. The empty ones below the lantern were fitted with ring bolts every sixteen inches. Less than three feet up was another shelf.

The slaves couldn't even sit up, thought Hamilton bitterly, *and they were chained so close together that a man couldn't rest on his back.* As he stared at the floating prison, he could imagine why many slaves had died.

The ship that had brought his mother to America twenty-three years earlier had been the *African,* under the command of Captain John Newton. His mother had often told him the story of the horrible "middle passage"—the stifling heat, the sickness, the despair. Rage boiled up in Hamilton's heart as he thought of what his mother had endured and what had become of his whole family since then. In addition to the hard, thankless work that only benefited his master and the periodic beatings for the smallest mistakes, there was always the threat that Bowdoin would sell him away from his mother and sister and the family would be broken up.

At the thought of Bowdoin, Hamilton decided he had better get up on deck and find the old man if he wanted to avoid his anger. The young slave made his way back down the walkway in the dark hold. Just before he went through the heavy door, he looked back at the gruesome sight revealed by the light of the swinging lantern. "Slave traders!" he swore under his breath. "If I ever meet the sea captain who carried my mother into slavery, I'll kill him!"

✧ ✧ ✧ ✧

When the *Hawthorne* dropped anchor in the harbor of Liverpool, England, three weeks later, Hamilton was definitely ready for dry land. The crossing was rough, and he felt slightly seasick most of the time. Actually, he was not certain what had made him most sick—the constant pitching of the ship or the foul smell in his master's cabin.

The old man hadn't fared well. He hadn't kept more than three meals down during the whole trip, and he had spent his entire time in bed in his cabin. Every few minutes he seemed to demand Hamilton's help, but he seldom knew what he wanted. "Bring me some water!" he would yell, and then a few minutes later, "Take away this putrid water, and give me some wine to settle my stomach." Then, "This wine is sour! I need brandy for my head. Can't you do anything right?"

Hamilton kept running the errands, but the worst part of his job was cleaning up when the old man got sick. The whole cabin stank so badly that every time Hamilton opened the door, he felt like throwing up himself.

Now he held Benjamin Bowdoin's arm as the old man tottered down the gangplank. Bowdoin's face was a pasty gray, and wisps of white hair stuck out from below his three-cornered hat. The old man sat on a bench on the wharf while Hamilton returned to the ship for his luggage. A hired carriage soon whisked them off to the Foxhall Inn—a large establishment with many rooms but poor service. Hamilton had to find the maid to get clean linens for the bed and water for the bedside commode. It didn't look as if anyone had cleaned the room for several days.

"Sir, should I get you something to eat?" Hamilton asked as the old man lay on the bed wheezing from exhaustion after climbing the stairs.

"No, no. I don't want anything. Just let me rest."

"But what about me?" Hamilton ventured. "I haven't eaten today."

"Well, go find yourself something. Just don't bother me anymore."

"But, sir, I have no money."

"Money? What do you need with money? Get out! Get out! Can't you tell when a body needs rest?"

Frustrated, Hamilton shut the door behind him and found his way down the back stairs. Here he was in a strange city in a strange country with a stingy master, and he had no idea how to find something to eat. Back on the plantation, slaves never had money of their own and never learned how to fend for themselves. What care they had came entirely from the hand of the master.

"And what can I do for you, young man?" asked the cook when Hamilton peeked in the kitchen door.

Hamilton had never heard a white person offer to do anything for him; he was so surprised that he almost darted back up the stairs. But the woman had spoken kindly. "N-nothin', ma'am . . . I was just a little hungry."

"Well, sit down here then, and I'll serve you up some rabbit stew." She gave him a knowing wink. "Those of us in service seldom have time to get a proper meal, now, do we?"

Hamilton was shocked. She was treating him as though he were an equal. He had never experienced such a thing from a white person.

The stew was thick and satisfying. After he finished eating, he went out the back door and through a narrow alley until he came to the street. It was late afternoon, and he had no desire to be back in the room with his complaining master. He walked along, lowering his gaze humbly so as not to offend the many white people on the street. But once, when the way was narrowed by a large barrel on the sidewalk, a white man stepped aside to let him pass first. Of course, Hamilton did not go first—that would have been impertinent—but it was a strange experience.

The only black person he saw that afternoon was

not showing respect

19

a finely dressed man riding in a carriage with a white man driving. Hamilton couldn't figure it out. The man didn't *look* like a slave. This was a very strange country.

Back at the inn, he poked his head into the kitchen before going upstairs. "Excuse me, ma'am," he said to the kindly cook, "but . . . are there any slaves in England?"

"Ain't we all slaves who's in service?" she snorted, vigorously beating a batter in a large bowl.

"No, I mean Africans, real slaves."

"Oh. Well, sure, there are a few, but not nearly as many as they have in the colonies, from what I hear tell. It sounds as if everyone over there has slaves. If that were true here, *I'd* be out of a job."

"Are there any African freemen here?" He was thinking of the man he had seen riding in the carriage.

"Umm, yes, a few. Say, now, you're from the colonies, aren't you? You sure speak like a Yankee."

"Yes, ma'am. I'm from Charles Town, South Carolina," Hamilton said. "Well, I best get on back up to the room. My master may be wanting somethin'. Thank you for the food."

But back in the room, Benjamin Bowdoin was still in his clothes, lying on his bed right where Hamilton had left him. It was getting dark outside, so Hamilton lit a candle. Bowdoin didn't move. In fact, he wasn't snoring his usual loud rattle.

Quietly, Hamilton carried the candle over to the bed and looked closely at his master. Something was wrong. There was no movement at all. The man wasn't breathing.

"Master Bowdoin?" said Hamilton quietly. But there was no reaction. He touched the old man's hand. It was cool—much too cool—and completely limp. Hamilton shook his shoulder. "Master Bowdoin, wake up!" he said more urgently. But his master did not respond.

Hamilton's eyes got large, and he jumped back. The old man was dead!

Chapter 2

A Thirst for Revenge

Panic punched Hamilton in the stomach. He had never been alone in the same room with a dead body. He ran to the door and yanked it open to yell for help—then stopped himself.

I gotta think, he told himself. *If I'm found with a dead white man—especially my master—I might be accused of murder. People will think I killed him!*

He closed the door quietly and went back to look at Benjamin Bowdoin. The old man's mouth hung open, and the flesh of his face had sagged like drapes of gray cloth around his jaws. Hamilton held the candle

23

close. Bowdoin had been dead only a short time, but he already looked different, almost unrecognizable.

Hamilton shuddered and backed away. What was he going to do? A mixture of relief and fear churned in his heart. On the one hand, he was finally free of the old tyrant. On the other, what if he got blamed for his death? "Back home a person could be lynched for less," he muttered. "I gotta get out of here."

It didn't cross Hamilton's mind that a doctor would be able to tell that Bowdoin had died from some natural cause like a heart attack. All he could think of was that he would be blamed. He had to get away!

The boy looked at Bowdoin's luggage. The old man owned many valuable things, but if Hamilton pawed through it, it would announce all the more loudly that he had been there. One thing, though, sat on the chair right beside Bowdoin's bed—a small satchel that the old man used for a purse and always kept with him.

Gingerly, Hamilton opened it. Inside were several coins—some gold—and a wad of paper money. There were several other papers and a pistol. Hamilton pulled out the pistol and looked at it in the candlelight. An idea grew in his mind. Now he had money, a way to protect himself, and an opportunity. *Why not run away?* he thought. *No one knows me, and it seems as if these English aren't so suspicious of a black boy out on his own. I might get pretty far.*

It did not occur to the boy as he tucked the purse under his arm that, though he was innocent of

Bowdoin's death, taking the purse made him a thief.

Hamilton waited in the room as the sounds of the inn finally quieted, well after midnight. When at last he felt sure the last guest was in bed and even the staff had turned in for the night, he picked up the small sack containing his personal possessions, checked to make sure that nothing else in the room betrayed his presence, then blew out the candle and stepped quietly to the door. Cautiously, he opened it. The hallway was dark and empty as he crept down the back stairs. The stairs creaked under his weight. He stopped, listened, then went on. The door was just ahead.

And then he was out in the narrow alley again.

Hamilton's first objective was to get as far away from Foxhall Inn as possible. Not knowing where else to go in Liverpool, he headed back toward the waterfront.

As he walked the dark streets quickly, he tried to plan what he was going to do. Maybe English people weren't on the lookout for runaway slaves. Maybe there weren't bounty hunters in England like there were in the colonies—men who made their living from catching and returning fugitive slaves for the reward money. But how could he know for sure?

Hamilton thought about his mother and sister on the Bowdoin plantation just outside Charles Town. He had to get home! But as he walked, it slowly dawned on him that he could never return home. If he showed up in South Carolina, he would be captured and returned to slavery immediately. In fact, if word got back about Bowdoin's death—no, make that *when* word got back—he might even be lynched.

Fear and worry knotted Hamilton's stomach. But how could he stay in England? He didn't know anyone here. There was no one he could trust, not even the cook back at Foxhall Inn. She had seemed nice enough, but that didn't mean she would protect him if she discovered he was a runaway.

His pace got slower as his mood got grimmer.

He was a long way from home in South Carolina—no! South Carolina wasn't *home.* If it hadn't been for that white sea captain who had taken his mother and father from their *real* home, he wouldn't be old Bowdoin's slave, and he wouldn't be in this terrible mess. *I'd be in an African village getting ready to go on my first hunt, or maybe I'd be training as a warrior, or climbing a tree to steal the sweet honey from a beehive.* He shivered, imagining the beestings he'd get for his efforts, but a smile tugged at his mouth as he recalled the stories of village life his mother had told him.

But that life will never be for me, he thought bitterly. He felt hot with anger again, the same way he had felt when he had found the shackles hanging from the beams in the hold of the *Hawthorne.* Somebody, someday, was going to pay for this.

His dragging footsteps finally brought him to the waterfront, and as the first rays of morning light began to illumine the harbor, Hamilton gazed at all the ships dancing lazily on the gentle swells. Something Mr. Bowdoin had said made him realize

Liverpool was home base for the shipping companies who financed the Atlantic slave trade. American goods came in, and English goods went out. The companies seldom had to dirty their hands with the third leg of their bloody triangle: human cargo.

I wonder if the African *is still sailing*, he thought. Twenty-three years before, when his mother had sailed on it as a captive, it had been a new ship. There was a good chance it was still in service—if it hadn't been wrecked in some storm or burned by rebellious slaves who succeeded in overpowering their captors—he had heard of such things happening. Hamilton began walking out to the end of each pier, inspecting the ships that were tied up and trying to read the names of those anchored out in the harbor. But the name *African* did not appear on any of the ships.

Was the *African*'s captain still alive? His mother had said Captain Newton had been just a young, brash man in his twenties. But that was years ago; there was a good chance he was too old to be at sea anymore. But he wanted to see what the man looked like—a man who could cram hundreds of men, women, and children into the hold of a ship while he walked freely about on deck. *If I ever see the man, I'll kill him!* thought Hamilton.

And then he had a jolting thought. Maybe Captain Newton lived right here in Liverpool.

Near a shed, Hamilton saw two scruffy-looking sailors sleeping on a pile of rope. They had nothing but a scrap of old sail over them to keep off the dew.

Then Hamilton noticed the empty rum bottle on the ground beside them and figured a couple of drunks would be as safe as anyone to talk to.

"Hey—hey, you, wake up," he said. "Wake up!" He pulled off their canvas blanket and kicked their boots.

" 'Eh, 'eh, not me, mate. Don't take me to sea again! I got the scurvy somethin' awful. See me gums?" And, without opening his eyes, the sailor pulled back his lips to show a toothless mouth with bleeding gums.

"Shut up, Jack," said the other man as he sat up and opened his eyes blearily. "It ain't no press gang." He squinted at Hamilton. "Why are you botherin' us, boy?"

Hamilton was alert, ready to run, but the two men made no move toward him, so he cleared his throat and gathered his nerve. "I'm, uh, looking for Captain John Newton. Do you know where he lives?"

"Never 'eard of him," mumbled the sailor who had sat up.

"He used to command the *African*, a slave ship that sailed out of Liverpool."

"Huh! I sailed to Africa five times," offered the toothless sailor.

"Not to Africa, stupid," said the other sailor as he found his hat and pulled it down over his eyes. "He doesn't want to know where *you* been. He's lookin' for a Captain Newton. Ever hear of him?"

"No, can't say as I 'ave." Toothless sat up. "But if you'd like me to look for 'im, I'd be glad to do so for a small fee, a veerry small fee . . . paid in advance, o' course." His eyelids drooped and he slurred his words almost beyond recognition.

"No thanks," said Hamilton and sauntered down the dock. Those two didn't know anything, but the conversation had given him courage. Until then he had felt that anyone who saw him would immediately know he was a fugitive. He felt as though he was wearing a big sign or something—but the sailors hadn't taken any notice.

Hamilton spoke with several other dockside bums without anyone recognizing the name John Newton. He was about ready to give up this foolish notion when he saw a salty old sailor mending a fishing net and smoking a little black pipe that he held upside-down between his teeth. Wouldn't hurt to ask again.

"Excuse me, sir, could I bother you a moment?"

The sailor looked Hamilton up and down and then squinted as a puff of smoke drifted into his eyes. "You want a job, boy? I need a hand on my fishing boat, and you look able enough."

A job? Fishing? Hamilton was tempted, but he had to get farther away from Foxhall Inn and the body of Benjamin T. Bowdoin.

"No, sir. All I want is some information."

"Well, I don't know much, but ask away."

"I'm lookin' for a Captain John Newton. Ever hear of him?"

"Captain John Newton, you say? Yep, I heard of him. He was the first man I sailed under." The man stood up and looked off across the bay as though he were looking into the distant past. "I crossed the equator with him for the first time back in '52—and was I lucky. Usually, when a man makes his first crossing, the crew treats him somethin' awful, an initiation, sort of. I've heard of blokes even dying from some of the treatment they give him. But Captain Newton wouldn't stand for no rough—"

"Excuse me, sir. Did you say that was in 1752? Did you happen to be sailing on the *African*?"

"None other, and she was a mighty fine guineaman, too. 'Twas her first time out, so we had it easy—not much scrapin' and scrubbin', if you know what I mean."

Hamilton's mind was racing. This man had sailed on the very ship that had carried his mother.

"What's the matter with you, boy? You look as if you've seen a ghost."

"Were there slaves on that ship?"

"Of course there were. That's what the *African* was—a guineaman, a slave ship. What's the matter with you, anyway?"

Hamilton was feeling the pistol inside Bowdoin's purse. Its smooth handle slid beneath the soft leather. He could pull it out and—but no. He wanted information, and this man was his first lead.

"Uh, sorry, sir. Didn't mean to . . . well, what I mean is, do you know where John Newton is now? Does he live here in Liverpool?"

"I wouldn't know. I been down in the South Seas for years with Captain James Cook. Only got back here last spring to buy me a little fishing boat. I figure that it's time for me to settle down."

"But haven't you even heard of Newton in the meantime?"

"Well . . . yes." The man scratched the stubble on his chin. "I heard that he quit going to sea and became the tide surveyor. But that was years ago."

"A tide surveyor? What's that?"

"You know, he takes his little boat out to meet all the incoming ships before there's a chance of them off-loading any cargo. He meets them at low tide, surveys the cargo, and sets the tax on its value."

"Does John Newton still do that?" Hamilton's voice rose in excitement.

"Nah. The government's got someone else doing it now. I don't even know the man's name. But you could go over to the office and ask."

The man pointed out the government office on one of the streets close by. Hamilton thanked the old man and headed eagerly away from the docks.

He was getting close.

But then he wondered, was it smart for a fugitive slave to walk into a *government* office and start asking questions—especially when just the night before he had left his master dead in his bed?

Chapter 3

The Captain of the *African*

The government office was a new-looking red brick building with white pillars. From a distance, Hamilton watched important-looking men go in and out. Many wore white powdered wigs and three-cornered hats. A naval officer with gold braids on his uniform and a long sword hanging at his side entered.

Hamilton hung back. He would certainly be conspicuous among such official people. And then a more common man—maybe a fisherman—walked in. If a fisherman had business with the king's representatives, why couldn't he? He would just have to make up some

excuse. Then it hit him. He'd been a slave; he would continue acting like somebody's servant.

While keeping his eyes lowered to avoid appearing uppity, he walked to the door as though he were on important business. Inside, Hamilton approached a clerk behind a polished desk. The man had his hair tied back in such a tight knot that it seemed to pull his eyes into little slits, and he held his pale lips in a similar thin line. Hamilton cleared his throat and said in his most proper English, "Excuse me, sir, but I have an important message for Captain John Newton. Can you tell me where I may find him?"

"Don't know a John Newton," said the clerk in a whiney voice without looking at Hamilton.

"But he's the tide surveyor."

"Not out of Liverpool." The man glanced up and frowned at Hamilton.

Hamilton's courage almost failed him. Had the man recognized him on the spot as the slave who left his master dead in the Foxhall Inn? Had word already gone out? But the man did no more than frown, so Hamilton again found his voice. "My master said that the last time he was in England, Captain Newton was the tide surveyor."

"Well, he's not now." The man clamped his lips tight and turned his head to speak to an older man seated at another desk in the office. "Mr. Weibolt, did we ever have a Captain John Newton as a surveyor?"

"That was eight years ago," said the older man.

The tight-lipped man in front of Hamilton

shrugged his shoulders and went back to his work.

Hamilton turned to the older man. "Could you tell me how to find him?"

"Hmmm. I think he moved to Olney. Heard he became the minister of the church there—which wouldn't surprise me none." The man snorted. "He used to preach to us around here enough."

Olney! He had the name of a town! Hamilton wanted to get directions, but both men had turned away and were ignoring him. He finally decided he shouldn't push his luck. He could find out where Olney was somewhere else.

A few questions of passersby helped him locate Olney. It was on the other side of England, a hundred miles away.

Hamilton sagged inside. Such a long trip seemed out of the question. He had never traveled anywhere alone in his whole life! But as he walked aimlessly down the street, he began thinking about the old fisherman who had sailed with Newton. The experience of actually talking to someone who had helped transport his mother across the sea burned within him and stirred his strange desire to see the man who was responsible.

Captain John Newton was living right here in England and had gotten away with a terrible evil. Now he was a minister, no less! What a hypocrite. He deserved to pay!

Hamilton felt the purse he carried over his shoulder. Within it was money—plenty of money to pay his fare on a coach to Olney. Why not? What else was he to do? Where else could he go? And Olney was a long way from Foxhall Inn.

By now he was getting pretty good at asking questions, and he soon found a coach going to Olney. Trying to look confident, he paid his fare.

"You understand," said the driver as he took Hamilton's money, "I don't go to Olney, just to Lincoln. You gotta get from Lincoln to Olney on your own."

"What do you mean?"

"Walk, unless you hire a horse."

"How far?"

"Oh, it's a good hike—twenty-five miles, I'd say. But there ain't no other way."

✧ ✧ ✧ ✧

After the coach dropped him off in Lincoln, Hamilton set out on foot to Olney, but nightfall found him with many miles yet to go. An old barn with clean hay was more appealing to the boy—and felt safer—than mingling with people in a local inn. Daybreak found him on the road once more, rested but hungry.

Long before he arrived in the town of Olney, Hamilton could see the tower of the church. The vicarage—the house the minister lived in—was next to the church. Several large shrubs filled the front yard and obscured the front of the house from the road. But down the circular drive, Hamilton could see a large, two-story building. Gables on the roof disclosed rooms in the attic.

Hamilton walked past the vicarage, glancing at the house without expressing any special interest, then he continued down the quiet, tree-lined street until he had passed several other large homes. Then he crossed over to the other side of the street and headed back. When he drew even with the church, a man came out and walked to the vicarage.

That can't be Newton, Hamilton thought. The man was small and rather odd looking. *He doesn't look like a sea captain. Maybe that man's a servant or something.* The idea troubled the boy. If Newton was not alone, how would he ever take his revenge?

Hamilton walked on past the vicarage, looking more closely at the building this time. Ivy grew up the walls and around the large windows giving the home an ancient look. Through one window, Hamilton could see the man moving around. He looked out the window, and Hamilton hurried on down the street so as not to attract any attention.

He walked around town for an hour or so killing time, then returned to the vicarage.

This time the man he had seen come from the church was sitting in a chair by the window reading. *Maybe that is Newton*, thought Hamilton, keeping out of sight behind some of the shrubs as he approached the old house. *It's either now or never.* Hamilton reached into the purse and withdrew the pistol. He would have to take his chances. If a servant answered the door, he'd use the gun to gain entrance. If it was Newton—well, he'd decide what

to do when the time came.

He stepped up to the door and tapped gently with the door knocker.

Nothing happened.

He rapped harder and heard movement within. Someone was coming. He held the pistol close to his chest and concealed it behind the purse.

The door opened. "Yes, can I help you?" It was the man Hamilton had seen walking from the church. He wore a black suit with a white ruffled shirt beneath.

"Is John Newton here?" Hamilton asked tentatively, looking back toward the street to be sure no one had seen him.

"I am he."

"You're John Newton?"

"Yes. What can I do for you?"

Hamilton was confused. This couldn't be the right person. The skin on his face looked sallow, not sunburned and tough like a man long at sea. Small bags hung under his pale blue eyes, and his gray hair was thinning. He did not seem as though he were someone who could command a crew of rowdy sailors.

But the man in the king's office in Liverpool had said that the captain had moved to Olney to become a preacher, Hamilton thought to himself. Then he quickly corrected himself. Technically, the man in the king's office had said that a "tide surveyor" named Newton had moved to Olney. Maybe two different people had the name of John Newton. Hamilton had not asked about a slave-ship captain. But at this point there was nothing to do but ask. Finally he blurted out, "Were . . . were you the captain of a slave ship called the *African*?"

"Well, yes," said the man in a soft voice. "But that was many years ago. Why do you ask?"

Hamilton stood in stunned silence. This was the man! This was the man who had carried his mother into slavery in the dirty hold of a slave ship. This man began years of torture and pain for his family. This man was responsible for misery beyond description for hundreds of Africans.

He let the bag fall away from in front of the pistol and raised it toward the man's face. "You . . . you," he croaked in a voice that shook with rage, "you chained my mother in the hold of your rotten ship, and . . . and—"

The words stuck in his throat. Pushing his way into the house, he kicked the door closed behind him.

Chapter 4

Tales at Gunpoint

The entrance hall to the vicarage was large, paneled with dark wood on the walls and black-and-white squares of marble on the floor.

"Is anyone else here?" Hamilton demanded, glancing up the stairway and down the short hall that ran to the back of the house. His heart was beating fast.

"No. Just me." Newton raised both arms in a gesture of innocence. In one hand he still held the book he had been reading, his place reserved with a finger between the pages.

Hamilton craned his neck to look into the side rooms. The one to the left was a library with a fire glowing on the hearth. "Aren't you married? What about servants?" the boy demanded.

The man was looking at him in puzzlement. "I am married, but my wife, Mary, is in London and won't be back until next Sunday. What is it you want?" When Hamilton did not answer immediately, Newton added, "We have no servants."

"You mean you take care of this whole place by yourself?" Hamilton sneered. The gun gave him confidence. He'd never talked to a white man like this before. "I've never known a white man to do that much work."

Hands still high, Newton shrugged. "A maid comes in twice a week—a church member who earns a little extra to help feed her children. We can use the help since we often have many guests and classes here on Wednesday evenings."

"Go back in there," said Hamilton, gesturing toward the library with his pistol. "But don't sit near the window. I don't want anyone looking in here and seeing you."

"I don't have any money if that's what you are after—at least not in the house and very little in the bank."

"I'm not lookin' for money. I got money." Hamilton nervously paced in and out of the library, looking up the stairs again and poking his head into the other rooms. He found it hard to believe that Newton was alone.

The minister watched the boy's nervous inspection with curiosity. "Well, if you're not after money, what did you come for?" The man pulled his chair near the fire and sat down.

"I came for you."

"For me?" Newton's eyebrows went up.

"Yes, you. You said you were the captain of the *African*, didn't you?" Hamilton looked around the library, noticing a globe in its stand on the floor and a sextant and a polished brass spyglass on the fireplace mantel. Above the mantel hung a painting of a three-masted ship. The small library did look to Hamilton as though it might belong to someone who had been at sea.

Newton eyed the boy. "I was indeed the captain of the *African*, and that painting you're looking at is of the same ship."

"The slave ship?" Hamilton stepped closer and stared.

"You know something about that ship, son?" Newton asked. His tone of voice changed slightly, as if he realized that Hamilton was personally connected.

Hamilton whirled around and pointed the pistol at the old captain. "You took my mother into slavery on that ship," he snarled. "I intend to kill you for what you did to my mother—and . . . and to all my people."

Newton didn't move, staring at the angry young man with the pistol pointed at his chest. Finally, the man tilted his head to the side and said with resignation, "Well, I guess I'm not surprised. The Lord knows I deserve it."

"What's that supposed to mean?" Hamilton

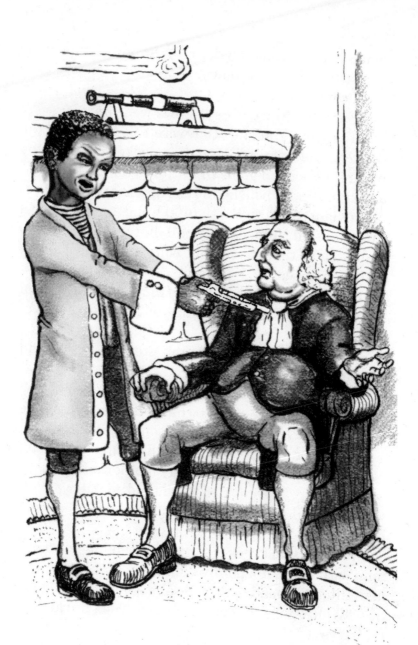

snapped. He was bewildered. The man was not re-
acting with fear as he had expected.

Newton put both hands to his face and gently
massaged his forehead with his fingertips. In a low
voice, he said, "The Bible says, 'For the wages of sin
is death, but the gift of God is eternal life through
Jesus Christ our Lord.' "

Nervously, Hamilton took a step toward the window and glanced outside. Satisfied that no one was
coming up to the house, he waved his pistol before
the old captain and laughed hollowly. "The wages of
sin is death, eh? You've certainly earned it, you
snake . . . and I'll be glad to pay it." Then he frowned
suspiciously. "But what's this talk about 'eternal
life'?"

Newton raised his head and rested his hands on
the arms of the chair. "Well, as you may understand
better than most people in England, the sins of my
life deserve more than death—they deserve eternal
damnation."

"What's that mean?"

"Hell, my boy. It means I deserve to burn in
hell—"

"Ain't that the truth!"

"Yes, yes, it's very true," Newton agreed, "but I
have confessed my sins to God—at least all that I
understand of them—and God has forgiven me and
released me from serving the eternal penalty I so
richly deserve."

"Huh! You think you can get out of it that easily,
do you? I don't know nothin' about the hereafter, but

you have certainly earned death here and now. God can forgive you all He wants, but He can't take that away from me. Your life is mine to take! What do you say to that?" Hamilton was so angry that his whole body shook. He wanted to see the man crying and trembling with fear. He wanted to hear him beg for mercy.

Instead, Newton shrugged. "What do I say about dying? Not much. The Bible says, 'It is appointed unto men once to die, but after this the judgment.' I know I shall die once—I'm just glad to know that on Judgment Day I won't be sentenced to the second death. As to when, I hate to disappoint you, young man, but that's not yours to determine. If you kill me, it will only be if God allows it. My life is in *His* hands."

"We'll see about that," Hamilton sneered. After all, he had the gun, didn't he? He stared into the captain's eyes. Newton said he knew he deserved to die—could that be true? Anyone could die of an illness, an accident, or old age. If killing the sea captain was going to give Hamilton any satisfaction, the man had to face the terrible things he had done. Did he understand that?

Hamilton wanted to rub the man's nose in his rotten deeds—so nicely hidden beneath his minister's garb. "So, you think you deserve to die," the boy mocked. "Then tell me why. I want to hear it from your own mouth. I'll just sit down here in this chair, and you can tell me."

Hamilton sat, still keeping the gun pointed.

"That's not hard to answer," Newton said. "It's because of the evil way I lived my earlier life."

"Yeah, yeah, yeah—but just what do you mean by that?" Hamilton wanted him to spell it out, every last rotten detail.

Again Newton shrugged. "Well, obviously you know I used to be a slave trader—that's why you're here. That was truly wicked . . . almost the worst thing I've done."

"Almost? *Almost*, you say? What could be worse?"

"That would take too long to tell."

"No. Tell me. I want to know," Hamilton said stubbornly. "What could possibly be worse than taking other people away from their families and homes and chaining them in the bottom of a ship to either die a miserable death or spend the rest of their lives in slavery? What could be worse? You have no idea what my family has been through! Or even what I have been through!" He was almost yelling.

"No, I'm sure I do not fully understand." Newton turned and gazed into the fire as though he were looking across the sea. Finally, in a far-off voice he continued, "You know, I was a slave myself once—almost died as one." He shook his head and looked back at Hamilton. "But you are right. I probably do not know how much pain I've brought you. Nevertheless, there was still one thing worse in my life, and it began when I was about your age."

Hamilton stared in astonishment. Newton a slave? It was hard enough imagining this thin little man with his gentle speech, soft face, and neat clothes as a vicious slave trader. Yet this man had practically admitted that he had put Hamilton's own mother in chains.

And what could be worse than being a slave trader? Hamilton had seen the terrors of slavery—vicious whippings, forced labor, broken families, even the death of his own father. Back in Charles Town, he knew slaves who didn't know where their own children were because they'd been sold to someone else, didn't know where their grandparents had come from because they had been brought over to America generations earlier.

"Go on," he challenged. "What did you do that was worse than being a slave trader?"

Newton smiled. "In order to tell you that, I'd have to tell you my life story."

Hamilton considered. He wanted to know what this man thought was worse than being a slave trader. Murder? No, slavery was worse than murder because the pain and misery went on and on and on. Nothing could be worse than buying and selling human beings for profit.

"You better get talkin' then," Hamilton said abruptly, waving his gun.

Newton looked surprised. "Would you like some tea? I could put the kettle on if you'd like." He gestured toward the black teakettle that hung from the arm mounted on the side of the fireplace.

Hamilton hesitated. He was both hungry and thirsty after his long journey from Lincoln. But was Newton trying to trick him? First he wanted to tell him a story, then he was acting as though Hamilton was a guest who dropped by for tea. *He's stalling,* thought Hamilton. *Maybe he expects some of his church people to arrive any moment and wants to keep me from taking my revenge until help arrives.*

"No. No tea. Just get on with your story."

"Well, suit yourself. But you don't mind if I have some, do you?" Before Hamilton could protest, Newton stretched out a leg and with the toe of his shoe swung the kettle over the fire. Then he began his story. . . .

Chapter 5

A Boy at Sea

My gentle mother—who taught me the Bible—died just before my seventh birthday. Life was pretty miserable after that. I feared my rough, sea captain father who had no idea how to raise children.

I took some hope when my father began courting another woman. At first she seemed interested in me, but as soon as they were married, I was sent off to a boarding school. Lessons began at six in the morning and went on until noon with only half an hour for breakfast. In the afternoon we worked for three or four hours.

Both the master and the older

pupils were very cruel. I remember the first time I was hit in the face. I was standing in line for dinner when one of the older boys came up to me and said, "That's my place."

I looked away, trying to ignore him. But he tapped me on the shoulder. When I turned back, he slugged me right in the nose. It knocked me back into the wall. I had never experienced such pain. Blood came pouring out, and I thought I was going to die.

The schoolmaster, who was coming down the hall and saw everything, walked past as though nothing had happened. Everyone else laughed.

I made no friends during my two years at boarding school and became more and more shy—and angry.

When I turned eleven, my father took me to sea for the first time. I welcomed the chance to escape the dreadful school and looked forward to getting to know my father, rough though he was. But when he wasn't busy barking orders to the sailors and running the ship, he spent all his free time writing letters to my stepmother, who had just had a new baby. I soon became convinced that he cared far more for that new baby than for me.

When my father did speak to me, he seemed displeased with my dreaminess and interest in books.

When I was twelve years old, something happened that shook me out of my sullenness . . . at least for a time. Between trips with my father, I was out horseback riding with a friend when we flushed a partridge from the grass beside the trail. The bird took off with such a roar that my mount reared up and threw me off. I landed on my back with a thud that knocked the breath out of me.

But as I gasped for air, I suddenly realized to my horror that I had escaped certain death by mere inches. Not just falling off the horse; there was no real danger in that. But someone had chopped down a hedgerow along the trail. The dried, pointed stumps of the tough little trees created a bed of sharpened stakes each twelve to fourteen inches tall. If I had landed on them, they would have pierced straight through me.

"That was a lucky escape!" my friend laughed as he rode off to retrieve my spooked horse. But the narrow escape meant more than that to me. For some reason, I realized, I had been saved. That night in bed I thought about God for the first time in years and all that my mother had taught me as a child. I sincerely believed the accident was not "a lucky escape" but "a second chance" to turn my life around.

There in the dark I vowed to behave better, to read the Bible like my mother had taught me, and to quit swearing like the sailors I had met at sea.

But in the morning, I forgot all about my promises and didn't even crack open the Bible. I joined my friends again in cursing God, doing as little as I could get by with, and in general wasting my life.

I continued in this fashion for the next couple years. Life did not make me happy. I was merely getting along with what came along.

One day, just before my fifteenth birthday, I arranged to visit a man-o'-war with my best friend and three other boys. The warship was anchored in the mouth of the Thames River, and we planned to meet early in the morning and use the outgoing tide to speed our trip out to the ship in a rowboat. But like the lazy fellow that I was, I slept in too long and had to run down to the water's edge.

When I got there, I was shocked to find that the other boys had left without me. They were out in the river, laughing and joking and clowning around as they rowed toward the ship. I yelled and cursed at them for twenty minutes, but they wouldn't turn back. "See you later, John Boy," they called back. "Fix us a pudding for when we return."

Furiously I stomped back and forth along the bank calling them every name I could think of. If I'd known how to swim, I would have dived in and headed after them.

But as I watched, a couple of the boys stood up in the boat—maybe to change places or something. Suddenly the boat began to rock as some unexpected waves hit it, and then in an instant it turned over.

All kinds of splashing followed as one boy after the other tried to find a grip on the slick, mossy bottom of the old rowboat. But as I watched, I could count only three who found a place to hang on. One was missing. From the distance, and with the waves splashing over them, I couldn't tell who it was, but the boys who were safe began yelling for help from the warship.

A boat was launched and the boys were rescued

before the tide carried them out to sea. That is, three boys were rescued—the three who could swim. My best friend, who—like me—could not swim, drowned.

I was shaken to the core, not only at losing my friend but because once again I had narrowly missed death. If I had been on that little boat and had been dumped into the water, I would probably have drowned, too.

The absence of my friend in the following weeks was a constant reminder that my life had been spared by Someone who had a purpose for me. But in my grief and self-pity I did not thank God for preserving my life. Instead, I cursed Him for letting my friend die.

From time to time I tried to reform, to turn back to God like my mother had taught me, but it never lasted long. Each time I was soon lying and cursing and being as selfish as ever. Even when I was trying to be "good"—as I thought of it—all I succeeded in doing was being gloomy and unsociable and useless. I lost all interest in living.

When my father came home from the sea, my stepmother complained, "You've got to do something with that wretched son of yours! All he does is lay around and brood all the time. It's driving me crazy."

So my father talked to a merchant friend of his who lived in Liverpool and arranged a job for me. I was to be employed as his representative and sent by ship to Jamaica—quite an opportunity for a boy of seventeen.

I agreed to the plan, but before I set sail, I went on a three-day trip to Kent to do some business for my father. While in Kent, I stayed with some of my mother's old friends, the Catletts, people my father had not bothered to keep up with.

The family had two girls, and from the first time I saw Mary Catlett, the oldest, I fell in love with her. She had creamy skin and dancing eyes, and my heart pounded every time she came into the room. She was just fourteen, but I knew it was true love, nonetheless.

Suddenly, I had something to live for. As a matter of fact, I was ready to do anything to see more of that girl. I decided there was no way I was sailing off to Jamaica for four or five years! But I dreaded telling my father, so I just stayed on with those friends for three weeks. By then the ship for Jamaica had sailed, and I had lost my job opportunity.

When I got back home, I made up a story for my father about being ghastly sick or something. Surprisingly, my father accepted it. I think he had feared that I had been drafted into the Royal Navy or attacked by highwaymen. In his joy at seeing me free and safe, he did not question my story too closely. Soon, however, he arranged for me to sail with another friend of his to Venice, a much shorter trip. This time I did not protest. A year's voyage to the Mediterranean was better than ten years of service in the Caribbean.

On that voyage I took up with a bunch of rough sailors and was soon drinking and swearing and visiting the fancy women in every port just like the rest of them—

✧ ✧ ✧ ✧

"Wait a minute," interrupted Hamilton as he leaned forward in the chair in Newton's library. "Are you trying to tell me that you were in love with a girl back home, but still you chased after other women when you were in foreign seaports?"

The tea water was hot, and Newton removed the kettle. From a small cabinet beside his chair he produced a cup, a spoon, a tin of tea, and a sugar bowl. He put a spoonful of tea into the cup and poured the water.

"That's right," the man admitted. "I couldn't seem to help myself. I had no willpower when it came to right and wrong."

Hamilton sneered. "Well, you were a rotten one, weren't you? But is that what you think of as a 'great evil' worse than being a slave trader? A little lying to your father . . . a little cheatin' on your girl—huh! That's nothing compared to chaining people in the hold of a ship and taking many of them to a living hell."

Newton added sugar to his tea and stirred thoughtfully. "Well, you're right about that. There's no comparison. Lying and cheating may not seem so bad to most people . . . but something else was beginning to happen. I told you this was a long story. You still want to hear it?"

Hamilton got up and went to the window. The afternoon shadows were lengthening, but he saw no one on the street. Then he went to the door of the

58

library and listened. "You expecting someone to come?" he asked suspiciously.

"No, this is Monday, my day off. I've asked people not to bother me on Monday. A minister needs some rest, you know."

"Well, nobody better show up. I'm telling you right now, if you're lying, I'll shoot them first."

"I don't expect anyone. But I can't make a promise. Sometimes there's an emergency."

Hamilton pulled nervously at the waist of his britches and returned to his chair, still keeping the gun pointed in Newton's direction. "All right, get on with it. You may be buying yourself a few more minutes on this earth with your storytelling—but it won't save your life."

Chapter 6

A Man of War

The trip to Venice was very different than any sea voyage I had been on before. I was no longer the privileged son of my father the captain. I was a common sailor scrubbing the deck and climbing the rigging like everyone else. I slept and ate with the common sailors and soon learned their rough ways.

Though I knew something about God because of my mother's training and had—on the occasions when my life had been preserved—gained an appreciation of God's care for me, I totally turned my back on Him. The captain held Sunday worship services on deck, but my

buddies and I mocked anyone who respected God in any way. The only time I felt any pangs of conscience for my behavior was when I thought of sweet Mary Catlett. I knew she would not mock God and would be shocked and ashamed of my behavior. But as much as I dreamed about her, that didn't restrain me.

During this voyage, war threatened between England and France, and the British navy was building up its forces. To get full crews for all its man-o'-war ships, "press-gangs" were often sent ashore to kidnap any able-bodied man they could grab. Most sailors dreaded serving on a naval vessel because the pay was so low and the discipline was so cruel—not to mention the very real chance of dying in battle.

The only seamen who were safe from being forcibly drafted into the navy were officers on merchant vessels, and even their papers were sometimes ignored. However, my father, with all his seafaring connections, arranged for me to sail as an officer on a merchant ship as soon as I arrived back in England.

It was a generous effort on his part, but I was too thickheaded to appreciate it. As soon as I arrived in England, I set off to Kent to visit Mary again.

I arrived just before Christmas—this was 1743, I believe—and again I hid from my hosts the fact that I was due to sail again in a few days. I stayed on enjoying the Christmas celebrations and other youth parties that Mary and her friends had. Near the end of January I finally returned to London—and, again, the ship my father had arranged for me had already sailed.

This time he was very angry. "Your stepmother is right! You're lazy and irresponsible—and ungrateful to boot. Well, that's the last time you're going to take advantage of my generosity. From now on I have no son."

His words stung me, but I shrugged them off. What did I care? Going to sea was all his idea anyway. I wanted to be free to visit Mary whenever I pleased.

But one afternoon as I walked along the docks thinking about going to Kent to visit Mary again, I was jumped by several men. Instantly, I knew my danger. They were a press-gang intent on making me a navy sailor.

I fought as hard as I could, but there were too many of them. They soon had me pinned to the ground with ropes around my wrists and ankles.

"I see by your checkered shirt that you're a merchant seaman," sneered the tall, dark-faced lieutenant who stood over me. "We need a few more men like you."

"You can't touch me!" I protested, spitting some dirt out of my mouth as I tried to catch my breath. "I'm an officer, with the papers to prove it."

"Oh? On what ship might that be?"

There he had me. If I named my ship, he would know that it had already sailed and I was a deserter. As a deserter, he could legally arrest me and draft me into the navy. If I did not name the ship, my claim to be an officer would be ignored, and he would draft me anyway.

I chose the latter route, hoping to buy myself some time to get out of this mess.

But in no time at all, I was aboard the H.M.S. *Harwich*, a 976 ton, fifty-gun man-o'-war requiring a crew of 350 men.

Finally, after my endless complaints that my father was a sea captain of significant standing in the world of shipping, I was allowed to send him a letter. The last time I had seen him, he had been so angry with me that he had disowned me, but it was my only chance. Life on a battleship was nearly as bad as being thrown into prison. In fact, the crew was largely made up of condemned criminals who accepted being sent to sea rather than swinging from the hangman's noose.

For a month, as the ship sat anchored in the harbor, I lived in the common quarters with the other draftees. We were overcrowded and fights were frequent. Below decks the rank smell and bad food made me constantly feel sick. In snow and rain we were forced to scrape the deck, caulk the hull, scrape and paint the masts, and sew new sails.

On April 3, Captain Cartaret called all sailors on deck and told us that England had formally declared war on France. I sank into despair; we would be sailing as soon as we got our orders. But two days later, the captain called me up to the quarter deck. "I have had a communication from your father, Captain Newton," he said bluntly. "I have decided to make you a midshipman. Go move your gear to an officer's berth and get a suitable uniform. Its cost will be deducted from your pay. That is all."

I thought myself very lucky and swaggered back past the other men with whom I had lived and worked for the last month. From now on they would have to treat me with the respect shown an officer, even though I was technically just an officer in training. To them I would thereafter be "Mister Newton"—or so I thought.

It did not take me long to take advantage of my new rank, ordering men around as though I owned them. "Get me some food!" "Polish my boots." "Clean up that mess"—even when I had been the one who had made it. I became intolerable and was hated by most of the common sailors.

But the rank of midshipman brought other privileges. I was no longer confined to the ship, so I often went ashore and visited Mary. My habit of returning late to the ship caused Captain Cartaret to distrust me. Each time he made me promise to be back on time, and each time I would be late. This went on for weeks as we awaited orders to sail.

When our orders came, the *Harwich* was not sent into battle against the French but assigned to escort merchant ships to Scotland and Norway, though once we did engage and defeat a French warship.

Then one day when we were back in port, we got word that the *Harwich* was to be sent on a year-long cruise. I had written Mary several letters, but she had never answered, and I was afraid of losing her. So I sent her a letter proposing to marry her when I returned.

I had not received an answer before we pulled anchor to join a large fleet of warships and merchant ships. Our route would take us down the coast of Europe and Africa, around the Cape of Good Hope, then up to India and finally the East Indies. I knew such a trip could mean we would be gone not one but five years.

We had no sooner assembled the ships and set sail when a terrible storm drove us back toward Land's End, the southwestern tip of England's rocky coast. Many ships were lost, and I was scared that we would be rammed and sunk in the dark night. Finally the storm blew itself out, and the following day those ships that were still afloat made it into Plymouth Harbor for repairs.

Repairs would take several weeks, and all I could think of as I sat on board was that to be gone from Mary for five years would certainly mean losing her to someone else. And I had not yet received her answer.

One day, the captain sent a long boat ashore to get supplies. I was put in charge and ordered to watch the men under me carefully. With such a long voyage before us, drafted crewmen were likely to desert.

But the moment we set foot on land, *I* was the one who took off. I didn't dare hire a horse or ask anyone for directions because if I gave any sign of not knowing my business, I would be suspected as a deserter. So I started walking across country.

I walked all day and all night, but the next afternoon a party of soldiers sent out to round up runaway sailors from some of the wrecked ships stopped me. I tried to talk my way out the situation, but I could not fool the officer in command. I was put in chains and marched back to Plymouth like a common criminal.

I spent two days in jail before Captain Cartaret sent for me to be brought on board ship. There I was again placed in irons below deck. I was a midshipman no longer.

A few days later I heard everyone being mustered on deck and wondered what was going on. Then the master at arms came to get me. I was a sorry sight, bedraggled, filthy, and hungry. As I stood on deck with the entire ship's company of 350 men watching, I thought the humiliation was punishment enough. But the captain glared at me and said stiffly, "John Newton, while being entrusted with a detachment of men on shore, himself deserted his post and was apprehended many miles away from here. Desertion while our country is at war can be punished by hanging. Therefore it is out of mercy that I sentence you to be flogged."

Before I realized what was happening, my shirt was stripped off and I was tied, spread-eagle, to a ship's grating.

"Give him the first dozen!" snapped the captain.

A huge boatswain's mate stepped forward and let loose with the first dozen lashes across my back with the cat-o'-nine-tails. Each lash was like fire! Before he was done, my back was a patchwork of red stripes.

Then a second boatswain took over with fresh energy for a dozen more lashes. As my skin gave way, I longed to pass out and escape the horrible pain. Finally, I did lose consciousness, and they cut me down from the grating.

In time, my back healed—though such whippings have killed many a man either from the trauma itself or the infection that often follows. But my spirit did not recover. I was reduced to the lowest possible status, scorned by everyone on the ship and without any protection of rank. In fact, the captain ordered that no one should befriend me.

A raging anger toward the captain infected my every thought. I wanted to kill him and planned several ways to do it. Fortunately, none of my schemes worked out. I also seethed with hatred toward my former mates who had turned against me.

I had never felt so alone.

But the hardest pain to bear was when we finally set sail and I was taken against my will farther away from Mary with the possibility of never seeing her again. I watched the English shore fade away behind us, and when I could see it no longer, I felt such despair that I nearly threw myself into the sea.

❖ ❖ ❖ ❖

John Newton paused in telling his story to watch his young captor. Hamilton Jones's eyes were drooping. "Maybe you have heard enough of my story," Newton said.

Hamilton sat up straight and blinked awake. "No, no. You keep going."

"You haven't told me your name."

"It's none of your business."

"Possibly not, but I've been telling you a lot of my business—the dirty business of my past. It seems only fair that I know to whom I'm telling it." He glanced at the bag into which Hamilton had replaced the pistol. "Especially if that person intends to kill me."

Hamilton thought a moment. It seemed like a reasonable request. After all, dead men tell no tales. "My name is Hamilton Jones."

"Hmm. I don't seem to remember anyone named Jones on one of my ships."

"Of course not," snapped Hamilton. "Jones is a slave name, given to my father before Mr. Bowdoin bought him and married him off to my mother."

Newton nodded. Then, as though changing the subject, he took a deep breath and said, "Well, Hamilton Jones, the afternoon is getting on. Would you like something to eat?"

Hamilton frowned uncertainly. He *was* hungry, but was this a trick? If they moved to the kitchen, would Newton go for a knife? Hamilton decided it wouldn't matter. With a gun, he was certainly fast enough to remain in charge of the situation.

"Yes. Get me some food!" he said as he stood up and waved his captive toward the door. Then he realized how much he sounded like the bossy young Newton in the story the man had been telling. No way did he want to be like this man! "I mean, you can get us both some food, but I'll be watching you, so don't try anything funny."

Chapter 7

Good Riddance!

It didn't take long for John Newton to prepare a plate of bread and cheese and pour two mugs of cider. As the man settled himself once more in the chair by the fire in the library under the watchful eye of the boy with the gun, Newton sighed. "Do you really want me to go on with this, lad? What difference does it make to you?"

"Huh! I haven't heard anything yet that sounds worse than being a slave trader." Hamilton paused. *I care nothing about this man,* he thought, *but for some reason* . . . "Yeah, go ahead. I at least want to know how you got from the bottom of the pile to

being a captain of your own ship." Not just any ship, either, Hamilton thought, but the ship that had carried his mother captive to a strange country.

"Well, I wasn't at the bottom yet!" Newton laughed ruefully as he took a swig of cider. "I was to sink even lower." He leaned back in his chair and continued.

✧ ✧ ✧ ✧

When the H.M.S. *Harwich* arrived at the Madeira Islands off the coast of northern Africa, we were in need of repairs. Apparently the storm off Land's End did more damage than we realized and we were taking on a lot of water. So the captain took us into a shallow harbor and set us to work. I was given the dirtiest jobs to do, scraping and taring in the noonday sun until my poor back that had only started to heal was covered with blisters even though I wore my rough shirt.

Everyone seemed to be picking on me, and probably they were, but I refused to admit that I deserved it. Instead I felt so sorry for myself that I was as uncooperative as I could be. After the ship was repaired, we stocked up on new provisions to make the long trip around the Cape of Good Hope at the southern tip of Africa. Oh, how I dreaded that voyage under such terrible conditions!

The day we were scheduled to set sail again, I was so tired that I didn't hear the boatswain's whistle call everyone up on deck. Job Lewis, one of the midshipmen, didn't want me to get in trouble so he tried to rouse me. But I got stubborn and picked up a book as though I was going to read it, even though it was too dark to read without a lantern. My rudeness angered Job, and he cut the rope suspending my hammock, and I fell to the floor.

He was actually trying to save my hide, but I was so angry that I wanted to kill him. Slowly, I made my way up on deck, the book still in my hand, and stood there sullenly as I watched a sailor throwing his gear into a small boat and rowing toward a nearby merchant ship.

"Hey, Job," I said as though nothing had happened between us, "where's that sailor going?" I should have addressed a midshipman as "Mister Lewis," but not me—I was too cocky and stubborn.

"What's it to you?" snapped Job, hurt that I was so ungrateful after his attempt to help me avoid trouble. But then he relented. "The captain needs a couple good carpenters to make sure this old tub holds together around the Cape, so he swapped a couple men with that Guinea ship."

Now, according to the Articles of War, the Royal Navy had authority over all British ships—still does, of course—so it was the captain's right to recruit any seaman he chose whether the man was engaged on another ship or not. It was only out of a sense of fairness that he arranged an exchange. But of course, I didn't see it that way.

"Sounds as though our greedy captain's lookin' out for himself," I said. "Two for one serves him well."

"It ain't that," said Job. "He intended to give two for two but at the last minute, he couldn't come up with another man he could spare."

Suddenly, opportunity filled my mind. I was headed for five years of misery on the *Harwich*, but a transfer to a merchant ship would get me out of the navy and land me back in England in no more than a year. I ran to the railing and yelled to the boat to hold up. Then I turned to Job and begged, "Get the captain to let me go! I'll go—then he can make an even trade. Go find him."

Job Lewis refused. "You know I can't do that. I can't walk in on the captain like that. You gotta go through the lieutenant on duty."

I ran off like a mad man, calling, "Lieutenant! Lieutenant!" When I finally found him and told him what I wanted, he just laughed at me. I must have looked as insane as I sounded: pants on crooked, hair all matted and wild, and eyes wide in my sunburned face.

Still, I begged and begged until finally he sauntered off to find the captain.

Whether the captain took pity on me or decided that this was as good a time as any to get rid of a troublesome, half-crazy kid, I'll never know, but the lieutenant came back and said, "Get your gear and be off with ya. And good riddance, too!"

I was over the rail and in that boat in an instant. I don't think anyone had ever seen me move so fast on that ship. I didn't take the time to get my hammock, boots, slicker, or anything. All I had was that

book in my hand—a copy of Barrow's *Euclid*, a geometry book. But I was gone!

Oh, was I proud of myself when I climbed aboard that merchant ship. I was out of the navy! I had a new start!—and what was even better, I'd be going back to England before long. Furthermore, once I explained who I was, it turned out that my new captain knew my father and therefore expected me to be a man of substance. He warmly welcomed me on board and made me a foremastman, a rank just below petty officer.

Oh, was I strutting. But as I watched the *Harwich* sail away I do remember realizing that my life had been saved once again. Not only had I escaped long-term misery, but as the lowest-ranking person on that battleship, I not only had to do all the dirty jobs, but most of those were also dangerous. It was me they sent up in the rigging first when the wind was blowing a gale. It was me who had to disarm a cannon that had misfired. It would have been only a matter of time before I slipped or had an accident.

There's a good chance that my transfer to that Guinea ship saved my life.

But I did not appreciate my good fortune for long. Pretty soon I was behaving worse than ever. I was lazy and abused those under my command, making enemies of them. I refused to take orders from my superiors and made up a song that mocked the captain. Pretty soon everyone was singing it—but not because they liked me for making such fun. No, most of the crew mistrusted me, knowing that I could turn on them as easily as I had on the captain.

Before we got as far south as the Cape Verde Islands, this captain, too, was ready to dump me in the sea—and he might have, too, had we not been so shorthanded. In addition to the captain and a couple mates, there were only about twenty-five crewmen. You see, we were a slave ship, the first one I had ever been on, full of men, women, and children—

✧ ✧ ✧ ✧

"Wait a minute," Hamilton interrupted, sitting forward on the edge of his chair. "You mean to tell me that after all you had been through—being in chains and thrown in jail, even being flogged—it didn't bother you seeing other people in chains?"

Newton nodded gravely. "I'm sorry to say that at the time it didn't bother me at all."

"But you *knew* what it was like to lose your freedom!"

"I knew it only as . . . as the way the world worked. It was just the way things were. There were people in power and people out of power. My only goal at that time was to never be without power again. I cared for no one but myself."

Hamilton's disgust for the man boiled in his stomach. "Some Christian you were—the Golden Rule and all that."

"I was not a Christian. Knowing *about* God and having been raised by a Christian mother did not make me one."

"Huh! I thought all white people were Christians. That's what they all say in South Carolina. Isn't England a Christian nation?"

Newton shook his head sadly. "I don't think there ever has been or ever will be such a thing as a 'Christian nation' until Jesus returns. There are certainly nations where Christianity is openly practiced and encouraged, and that's a good thing. But it doesn't mean that everyone is a Christian, and it certainly doesn't mean that all the attitudes or practices of those people are godly. We all start with the attitudes of the world we are born into and learn God's ways slowly. Only when we seek Him with open hearts do we truly change. I was a long way from having an open heart. Remember this," Newton said, wagging a finger at Hamilton, "Christian *is* as Christian *does*."

Hamilton turned and stared at the coals of the dying fire, thinking about what Newton had said. Hamilton had known some pretty good people among the other slaves, and others who only pretended to be good—"hypocrites," his mother had called them. He had even heard of a few white people who opposed slavery, but back in South Carolina he had never met one—not even one.

Hamilton recalled his former master, Benjamin Bowdoin, always went to church. "If Christian is as Christian does," he challenged Newton, "can a slave owner be a Christian?"

John Newton rubbed his chin thoughtfully. "Christian behavior means acting like Christ. It is not Christlike to treat another human like property. Therefore slavery is not Christian behavior even if a Christian owns slaves. But whether any specific slave owner is a Christian or not, that's God's business to judge, not mine. The Bible says all of us have sinned and fall short of what pleases God."

"Huh! Here you are—a minister, they say. How can such a scoundrel as you call yourself a Christian?"

The challenge hung in the air. The evening chill was creeping into the house, and Newton got up and put an oak log on the fire before he answered.

✧ ✧ ✧ ✧

On board that slave ship was a man named Clow who was returning to his home on one of the Plantain Islands off the west coast of Africa. Though this man had started out very poor, he had become rich through the slave trade. He bought slaves from the native kings and traders on the African mainland and held them on his island to sell to passing ships.

The captain of our ship bought several slaves from Clow, and I admired his island operation because it was too far from the mainland for anyone to escape. I began thinking that I'd like to get rich, too, and might someday join in the same type of business, maybe on an adjacent island.

When we had our quota of slaves and were about to set sail across the Atlantic on the dreadful Middle Passage to the West Indies, however, our captain took sick with tropical fever and died very suddenly. This happens to many white men in that region.

That meant the command of our ship passed to the first mate. He was a no-nonsense sort of fellow who had me figured out. I knew he hated me and would look for any opportunity to get rid of me. What I feared most was that he'd trade me to the first Royal Navy ship we'd encounter, and then I'd be back where I'd started.

That's when my greed and my fear joined forces to hatch a new plan. I suggested to Clow that I'd be glad to work for him if he could arrange my leave from the ship. I was too eager to get off the ship to ask about the terms of my employment and left it to him and the first mate to come up with something to satisfy them both.

And they did.

I was given over to Clow with no limit on the length of time I was to work for him and no agreed-upon wages for my service. Essentially, I had no more rights than a slave, but I left the ship as cocky as a bantam rooster. I expected to turn it all around and return to England a rich man.

As we rowed toward Clow's island fortress, he turned to me and said smugly, "You will work for my wife. She's African and will get no end of satisfaction out of showing off her British servant to the native kings and traders who come to visit." And Clow threw back his head and laughed.

Chapter 8

A Slave to Pea Eye

Hamilton jumped up from his chair. "You were a slave to a black woman?" he exclaimed, and then he started to laugh. At first it was just a chuckle, but what a strange twist of chance! This man, who had carried his African mother into slavery, had himself been the slave of an African woman. Maybe there was a little justice in the world after all!

"Tell me," he said when he had caught his breath, "surely she treated you much better than the slave masters in America treat us."

"Possibly . . . possibly. But I have no way of comparing. I have not been to the colonies. But I can tell you what happened to me . . . if you're interested."

"Of course," said Hamilton as he sat back down. "I want to know about my people, about my country. What was it like?"

So Newton continued.

✧ ✧ ✧ ✧

Clow had built a substantial log house on the island and had begun planting groves of lime trees to sell limes to the Dutch. The Dutch believe that limes prevent sickness among sailors.

When we landed, a whole crowd of people came down to welcome us. They were all Africans. I had not seen very many black people before we took the slaves on board ship, and many of those were straight from the bush, scared, and disheveled. But the Africans who met us on the island were impressive. They were part of Clow's household—his servants, field hands, and even his wife.

She walked among the others as though she were a queen. She was tall and very beautiful with smooth skin and sparkling eyes and much gold jewelry. Later I learned that she was a princess in her own tribe and had been very important to Clow's success as a trader by influencing many mainland kings and tribal chiefs to trade with him.

"This is John Newton," Clow said, introducing me to his wife. "Newton, this is my wife, Pea Eye."

She looked at me briefly and then turned away as though I was nothing more than some half-drowned cat that he had brought ashore with him. All she was interested in were the chests of fancy gowns and jewelry he had brought for her from England.

"Clow," she said in very good English after she had inspected the treasures, "take these things up to the house and have them put away for me." Clow quickly obeyed, and I began to realize that *she* was the person in charge on this island.

I followed along with my few personal belongings—which included my geometry book—while Clow directed the servants to make fast the boat and carry the chests to the house.

I entered the house behind Clow and was waiting for him to show me to my room when Pea Eye took her first real notice of me. She frowned and said, "What's he doing here? Send him out with the others." At that moment I knew I was in for trouble if I didn't get on her good side.

"Out with the others" meant a line of round mud huts with thatch roofs and dirt floors. I assumed they were typical of the houses in most African villages. These people were Clow's personal servants and field hands, not the slaves he sold to the ships. The slaves for market were kept in a large fortlike stockade, and since most of them had recently been put aboard ship, it was almost empty.

I had a hut to myself, and didn't find the accommodations too bad, especially after being cramped into a small hammock on board a ship for so long.

I saw nothing more of Clow until that evening when he came to get me for dinner. The other servants were preparing their meals over open fires, so

I figured Clow had made some headway in convincing Pea Eye to accept me into the house since dinner there was obviously not for "the help."

The meal was excellent, the best I had had in months, and Clow spoke to me pleasantly enough. But Pea Eye didn't say one word to me.

The next day I felt ill and stayed in my hut. Food and water were sent to me, though I wasn't very interested. I got worse, and the following day Clow visited me with a worried look on his face. "You've got the fever," he said as though I didn't already know it. "I won't be able to stay with you. I've got to make a trip up river. I'll be gone close to two months. But Pea Eye will take care of you."

I had my doubts about her care, but I felt too weak to protest, and I was certainly in no shape to go on a trip up a jungle river. I had heard that many white men died of tropical fever, and all I hoped was that I didn't do the same.

By the next day, I was nearly out of my mind with the fever—sweating one minute and shaking with chills the next. I passed out for long periods of time. Once I remember coming to with Pea Eye standing over me. "Water . . . water," I begged, but she only laughed and walked away. She brought me no food, and I'm certain I would have died had not some of the household servants shared a little water and food with me when Pea Eye wasn't around.

This went on for many days, though time meant nothing to me because I was out of my mind for most of it. Then very slowly I began to experience longer periods of time when I was in my right mind. But I did not *feel* better. In fact, I felt worse and was certain that I was dying, but some of the servants assured me that I was over the worst part and would get better. "Your spirit almost gone before," they would say, shaking their heads.

Again I had been saved from dying, and sometimes at night the question tickled my mind: *Why? Why have I lived when others have died?* I knew that Christians believed that God is in charge of life and death, but I rejected that idea because it suggested God had preserved my life for some purpose, and I didn't want to face that possibility. I didn't want God to have a purpose for me. I didn't want to deal with God at all.

One day Pea Eye brought a plate with a little food on it, but she would not hand it to me. Instead, she put it on the ground as though she were feeding a dog and laughed at my efforts to crawl over to it. Each time I got a bite or two, she would kick it away, making me crawl some more.

When I was strong enough to stagger out of my hut, I asked her why she treated me so badly. "I do not want you here," she said honestly.

"Why not? I have done you no harm."

"You are European," she spat. "You remind my husband of England. Maybe someday he will go back to England and leave me alone." Then she walked away.

Finally, I began to understand her hatred of me. I threatened her security, her comfortable way of life.

She lived like a queen, but if Clow left and there were no more shipments of goods from England to trade with the kings and chiefs, she would be nothing. Furthermore, though she had been important in setting up Clow's business, it was at the expense of betraying many African people into slavery. Families and friends of those people would have liked to take revenge on her. So she was not safe without Clow.

But understanding Pea Eye's reasons for hating me did me no good. Nothing I did helped me get on her good side.

When Clow finally came home, I was back on my feet, though still a little weak. He had had a successful trip and was in good spirits, and I hoped we could proceed with developing a business relationship. But Pea Eye kept telling him that I was a cheat and intended to steal from him. At first he didn't believe her, but like any lie, the more often it was said, the more believable it became. Clow began to behave cautiously around me, not leaving me alone in the room with his business record books or giving me any responsibility.

During this time I worked in his lime grove planting new trees along with the other field hands— often under Pea Eye's scowling gaze. Then one day he had to go on another trading expedition and told me that I was to come with him. I thought he was finally beginning to trust me. But I am afraid he just wanted to keep a closer watch on me because of his growing suspicion.

We were several days up river in his boat when we met another European trader. Clow invited the trader onto his boat and they drank most of the evening until Clow was so drunk that he passed out. The next morning a case with six muskets in it which had been brought to trade for several slaves was missing. It was clear to me that the stranger had stolen them, and I suggested that possibility to Clow. But when he confronted the man, the man became upset and started yelling, "Me? How could it be me? Who gave you that idea? Oh, friend, how could you suggest that of me, a fellow trader? We have worked these rivers for years together. Does that not prove my good will? Some evil person must have put that idea into your head."

Clow didn't answer, but his gaze briefly drifted toward me as I sat in the back of the boat.

Seeing it, the other trader turned to me. His eyes got large, and with fake sincerity he said, "No. I wouldn't believe it of the lad. But . . . could it be that he is trying to cover his own sin? Has he betrayed you?"

And that was it. By that age I had committed almost every other evil possible, but I was not a thief. However, there didn't seem to be anything I could say or do to clear myself. With the suspicions that Pea Eye had planted in Clow's mind and then the wild declarations of the real thief, Clow believed I was guilty.

Clow was so angry he threatened to shoot me on the spot. And he might have done so had not a convoy of canoes come around the river bend at that moment. The natives paddled their canoes in time to a drum beat and a rhythmic chant by the warriors who were decked out in elaborate paint and feathers. In the center of each canoe were three or four captives tied together with strong vines.

The captives were being delivered to Clow in

exchange for his treasures.

The negotiations on the price for each slave were difficult, especially since Clow was missing the muskets he had promised the chief. The muskets were to make the chief more powerful and protect him from retaliatory raids from the tribes from which he had taken prisoners. Without them, his people were in great danger.

Finally, after softening up the chief with an excessive amount of rum, Clow was able to make a deal for the best prisoners—he wanted only the young able-bodied people.

Once the prisoners were confined to wooden cages on board his boat, he pulled anchor and retreated downriver. I heard him say, "When that chief sobers up and discovers that all he got for his slaves were some machetes and a few bolts of cloth and a small barrel of watered-down rum, he's going to be very angry. Newton," he glared at me, "you may have lost me one of the prime places of trade. I won't dare come back here for a long time."

At the mouth of the river was a small settlement, and Clow left his new slaves imprisoned there in a warehouse to be picked up later. Then we sailed farther south to the next river.

But by then I had discovered my fate. Whenever Clow left his boat, I was chained to a ring fastened to the deck. It was the same kind of ring used aboard other slave ships. During the Middle Passage a few slaves at a time would be brought on deck during the day for some fresh air. They would be chained to the ring so they couldn't cause any trouble or jump overboard.

✧ ✧ ✧ ✧

Hamilton interrupted Newton's story. "Wait a minute. If a ship was in the middle of the Atlantic Ocean, why would a slave jump overboard?"

Newton rubbed his head in his hands. When he looked up at the young African, a pained look was on his face. "Many of these slaves were a proud people. The idea of being taken from their home to be slaves in a far-off country upset them so much that they preferred to die rather than face that future."

"So they would jump into the sea?" asked Hamilton.

"Yes, or try to end their life some other way."

"Like how?"

"By refusing to eat."

"Did they die from that?"

"Seldom . . . very seldom. We wouldn't let them."

"What could you do?"

Newton looked out the window. "I don't think you want to know about this. Let's get back to my story."

"No. Tell me. Tell me everything!"

Newton shook his head slowly.

Hamilton reached into his bag and pulled the pistol out again and pointed it toward the man. "I said, tell me."

Newton sighed. "We had this wedge—mind you, this didn't happen very often—anyway, we had a wedge that we could force between a slave's teeth. It was split in half with a screw. When we turned the screw, the two halves would open up, forcing the person's mouth open enough for us to get some food down them." He paused. "We really didn't want people to die."

"Of course not!" sneered Hamilton. "And I know why. Dead slaves didn't bring you any money. It was just a matter of money for you and your ship owners, wasn't it?"

"That's right. Just money." John Newton got up to stir the fire, and then continued.

✧ ✧ ✧ ✧

I was never allowed below deck even though the monsoon rains had begun. My only shelter was under a makeshift tent of old sailcloth. My food rations were cut to one pint of rice per day—when Clow remembered—and any fish I could catch.

Every time Clow left his little ship, he chained me to the ring, which was too far from my tent for shelter and too far from the side of the boat to fish. My only clothes were a ragged shirt, a pair of trousers torn off at the knees, and a handkerchief instead of a cap. In that condition I endured twenty, thirty, even forty hours of hurricane-force storms while Clow was away on shore.

Often my fever came back, and I thought I was going to die.

When we finally returned to Clow's island, Pea

Eye assigned me to work with the field hands clearing the jungle and planting lime trees. But before I was sent out to the fields, Pea Eye took me to the blacksmith's shop and had a pair of ankle-irons put on me. "To keep you from escaping," she laughed, as though there was any way to get off that island. Later, in the fields under the hot, tropical sun, the African overseer used his whip on me as freely as on the other slaves. I was just another of Pea Eye's slaves.

One day when Clow and Pea Eye came out to inspect the fields, Clow mocked me. "Who knows? Someday you may make a fortune and come back when these trees are grown and reap the fruit of your labor."

Pea Eye laughed long and hard at that. Finally, she had me where she wanted me—a common slave who was no threat to her little kingdom.

Chapter 9

Rescue

Hamilton got up from his chair and went to the window. It was dark outside, and all he could see were a couple lights from the windows of houses across the street. In the residential neighborhood where John Newton lived there were no streetlamps.

He turned around with a start to look at his captive sitting in the firelight. He was getting careless. Newton could have snuck up behind him with a fire poker and hit him over the head. But . . . somehow Hamilton knew there was no danger of that. Even though the old sea captain had carried the boy's people into slavery, Hamilton had started to trust

the man sitting here in the vicarage library. Could this gentle man be the evil monster Hamilton had imagined him to be? If not, what had changed?

"Can we have some light?" he said nervously. "It's getting dark in here."

"Of course," said Newton. He poked a straw into the fire, then with the burning ember lit a lamp on the mantel and another on a small table.

As Newton turned the wick screw and the lamps glowed brightly, Hamilton mused, "From your story, I guess you do know what it's like to be a slave. But if you knew how awful it is, how could you ever do that to other people? How could you send other people into slavery?"

The minister shook his head. "Knowing pain is seldom enough to keep a person from passing it on to someone else. Have you ever watched chickens?"

Hamilton nodded. "Of course. We've got plenty on the plantation. I used to have to feed them every day."

"Well, then you may have noticed that the strong hen or rooster will peck on the weaker ones, chase them away from the corn or the freshly found worm. But are those weaker ones nice to each other because they don't like being pecked on? Never! They will just pick on the next weaker bird."

Hamilton almost laughed. He'd seen chickens act like that, all right.

"Humans are the same way," Newton said. "We pass along the evil that has happened to us—unless something turns us around."

"Turn people around? Huh! What can do that?"

"Sit back down, and I'll tell you."

Hamilton returned to his seat across from the captain, his hand still loosely on the pistol in his lap, and Newton continued his story.

✧ ✧ ✧ ✧

I was a miserable slave on that island for nearly a year. My only possessions were the tattered clothes on my back and my geometry book. On the rare occasions when I was not working in the fields or so tired that I immediately fell asleep, I would take my geometry book down to the beach and draw diagrams in the sand. I had no friends, and this was my only diversion to keep me from going crazy.

Clow would not let me visit the ships when they called to purchase slaves from him. He knew that it was not legal for one Englishman to keep another one as a slave, so he would confine me to some distant part of the island away from the small harbor where the various ships' boats usually beached.

But I managed to get one of the African servants to get me some paper and a pen from Clow's house, and with it I wrote a letter to my father in England, explaining my condition and begging for his help. That same sympathetic African smuggled it on board the next English ship that arrived, and I waited anxiously for some response, hoping I would be alive months later when and if help arrived.

When the time came and went that the first

possible response might have come from my father, I wrote another letter, thinking the first had been lost.

Then one day, another English trader moved onto the island, building himself a house on the other side. Pea Eye disapproved strongly, but Clow was eager for the company of another white man—a role he had hoped I would fill.

Of course with the man living on the island, there was no way to keep me out of his sight, and upon noticing that I was treated as a slave, this newcomer expressed surprise to Clow. "Oh, he's not a slave," said Clow. "He's a servant we hired, but he stole some muskets from me, and so he's being punished."

However, as time went on and my "punishment" continued, the man got suspicious. One day he came across my geometric drawings in the sand and realized that I was an educated person and told Clow that he wanted to meet me.

I guess that worried Clow, causing him to think that he might get in trouble for enslaving a white person. I actually happened to be within earshot of this conversation and heard Clow say, "You are alone and new to this island. I'm sure you could use some help. Why don't you give the boy a job? I can't seem to handle him very well, but you seem . . . well, more experienced."

Whether the new trader was flattered by Clow's words or was eager to help me, I'll never know, but the transfer was made, and I went home with a new boss that very night.

How wonderful to have soap to wash with and

clean clothes to put on for the first time in over a year!

Again I had been saved from possible death. The treatment under Clow and Pea Eye was so cruel and the tropical climate so severe—with its unbearable heat and heavy monsoon rains—that I could have lapsed back into a deadly fever at any time.

This new trader listened to my story and for some reason believed me, especially when I showed that I was willing to work hard for him and help him in his business. We traveled up many of the rivers trading for ivory, wood carvings, precious stones, and—of course—slaves.

After several months of this life, I had nearly forgotten about the letters I had sent to my father and my "need" to be rescued. Life had greatly improved, and there was the possibility of going into partnership with the new trader or even establishing myself on my own. With a comfortable life, slaves to do my work, and exciting trips into the interior, I began to think of myself as happy.

But my father had been busy. He told Joseph Manesty, the owner of a shipping company, that he would pay a reward if any of his captains found and returned me to England. One of them, the captain of a ship named the *Greyhound*, was determined to collect the reward and had been asking for me at every port up and down the west coast of Africa.

It so happened one afternoon that the *Greyhound* was sailing past our coast at just the time we needed more trading supplies. So we set a fire to create a smoke signal and attract attention. Slowly the ship came about and dropped anchor. When the ship's boat brought the captain ashore, he was delighted to find me and invited me to come aboard with him.

Surprisingly, I wasn't so eager to leave Africa. My dreams of getting rich had revived.

"Haven't you heard?" said the quick-thinking captain, who didn't want to forfeit his reward. "Your uncle died and left you an income of four hundred pounds silver per year?"

Well, that was different, I thought. On that much money I could live very well, and though I couldn't imagine which uncle might have left me so much money, it was enough to convince me to return to England. So I left on the *Greyhound*.

The *Greyhound* was not a slave ship but transported gold, ivory, dyer's wood, and beeswax. It had not yet collected all of its cargo, so we sailed on south, stopping at other ports of trade. I grew bored with this delay in returning to England and by this time forgot the misery I had escaped under the wrath of Pea Eye and Clow.

My old, sour attitude returned. I felt no gratitude to God for saving me—much less to the captain of the ship—and I became arrogant at being forced to "waste" so much time aboard the *Greyhound*. I began to make more and more of a nuisance of myself and encouraged the crew to be troublesome, too. One night as the ship was anchored in the mouth of the Gabon River, I persuaded four or five sailors to join me in seeing who could drink the most rum before passing out. It wasn't long before my brain was fired

up, and I got up and danced around the deck as if I were a madman. My hat flew off and fell into the water.

I looked over the edge and started to dive in when one of my buddies grabbed my shirt and pulled me back. Once again, my life had been saved. I can't swim *and* I was very drunk. The current in the mouth of the river was very swift, and I certainly would have been pulled away by that tide and drowned.

To return to England we had to catch the same trade winds that the slave ships used, going west across the Atlantic near the equator, sailing up the eastern coast of America, and then sailing east with the winds across the northern Atlantic to the British Isles.

During this trip, my attitude got worse and worse. I guess I was hoping the men would find me amusing, but I think I just made them hate me. Sailors are often a superstitious group, and while they swear and curse freely, there is a limit on what they think God will allow. I often crossed that limit, mocking God by saying things like, "If there's a God, let Him strike me dead as I stand here on this accursed ship." As a child my mother had taught me many Scripture verses, but on the *Greyhound* I twisted them in mockery of the Bible, Jesus, and God himself. Once, when a rough storm was blowing up, I stood at the ship's railing yelling, " 'Peace, be still,' " as Jesus had done when He rebuked the wind and waves and calmed the sea. When the storm continued, I said something like, "Guess the Old Man ain't listenin' to me today."

Such terrible blasphemy shocked and scared the crew because they expected God to strike me dead with a bolt of lightning.

❖ ❖ ❖ ❖

"I can't believe you did that," Hamilton interrupted. "It *is* a wonder God didn't strike you dead right there and then."

Newton's face was sober, but the beginnings of a faint smile brought a twinkle to his eyes. "Why do you say that?" he asked.

"That's obvious!" snorted Hamilton. "It's not just what you said—that's outrageous enough. It's—it's the whole way you lived. All you lived for was yourself. You were so . . . so selfish, so ungrateful."

"Ungrateful?" said Newton, raising his eyebrows as though he was amazed at Hamilton's comment. "Why should I be grateful?"

Now it was Hamilton's turn to look astonished. "*Why* should you be grateful? Don't you understand? Can't you see it? You had a decent home, you had privilege, you had a mother and father who cared about you—and you just threw it all away. Then God saved your life again and again, but you paid no attention to Him. No, worse than that. You cursed God and mocked Him. That's rotten. That's about the worst thing I can think of."

"Are you sure? Worse than being a slave trader?"

"Huh! Slave trading was what you *did*. This is what you *were*—rotten to the core!" Hamilton spat out the words in disgust.

"You're right," said Newton. "I think you're starting to understand."

But before Hamilton could respond, a sharp knock sounded at the front door of the house.

Chapter 10

Homeward Bound

Hamilton jumped. The knock at the door sounded again.

Startled, the boy reached for the bag that held his pistol. It had slid out of the chair and fallen to the floor. *What a fool I've been,* he thought. *I should've known this was going to happen. Newton set a trap for me, keeping me talking until someone came to rescue him.*

"Don't answer it," he hissed in a whisper as he pulled out the pistol.

"I must answer the door," said Newton calmly. "The lamp is lit. Whoever it is will know that I'm at home."

"No! Maybe they'll just think you left it on while you went out."

Newton closed his eyes and shook his head briefly, indicating that the idea would never work. He stood up slowly with his hands out before him, palms facing Hamilton. "Let me go answer the door. It'll only take a minute, and I'll tell whoever it is that I'm busy."

"No!" said Hamilton again as he raised the pistol. But Newton kept walking. Part of Hamilton's brain said, *Now! Or you'll miss your chance to kill him!* But the boy hesitated. There was something about the man's frankness that was getting to him. Whatever Newton had been, *something* had changed him deeply. Could he really pull the trigger on the man now?

The knock came again. Suddenly Hamilton dropped the pistol on the chair, stepped quickly across the room, and hid behind the heavy blue drapes that hung beside the window. He heard Newton open the front door and say, "Well, good evening, Mr. Fielding."

The other person's voice was indistinct, but in a moment Newton answered, "No. This evening wouldn't be a good time. I'm quite busy with a . . . a personal matter."

The visitor said something else.

"Oh, you know," responded Newton with a chuckle, "Monday's my day off. Why don't you stop by tomorrow evening? Then I'd be glad to go with you."

After a moment, he said, "Good. I'll look forward to it. Goodbye, then."

Hamilton heard the door close and Newton's footsteps walking into some other part of the house. He had a strong urge to go after him. What if his prey was escaping? But for some reason, Hamilton stayed put, thinking about Newton's strange story.

In a few moments, Newton returned to the library, and it was only then that Hamilton remembered with a panic that he had dropped his pistol on the chair.

The sound of Newton's footsteps with an occasional creak of a floorboard indicated his slow movement into the library. *By now he can see the pistol,* thought Hamilton. *But he's not so young; maybe I can still make a dash for it and grab it before he reaches it. Oh, why did I leave it there?*

"Mister Jones," said Newton softly. "Mister Hamilton Jones, have you decided to leave me before I finish my story?"

Was he picking up the gun? Hamilton stayed put, holding his breath.

Newton's chair squeaked as the older man took his seat.

Finally, Hamilton peaked out from behind the drape. Newton was looking right at him.

"Well," said Newton mildly, "are you going to sit back down?" He tipped his head and looked toward Hamilton's chair. "Or do you want to hear the rest of the story from behind that drape?"

Hamilton glanced at the chair. The pistol was still there. *He's seen it!* thought Hamilton. *Why didn't he grab it and get the drop on me?*

"Sorry for disappearing for a minute," said Newton as Hamilton eased his way out from behind the drapes. "But after drinking all that tea, I had to"—he waved his hand vaguely—"answer the call of nature, so to speak. Now, come on, sit down . . . sit down. We were just getting to the good part of my story."

Hamilton crossed the room, scooped up the pistol, and sat down as though nothing unusual had happened.

"Now," said Newton, "I had just mentioned how outrageous my attitude had become as we were sailing up the east coast of America.

✧ ✧ ✧ ✧

We spent some time fishing for cod off the coast of Newfoundland. Then we turned east toward England and home. The ship had been at sea so long that it was in poor condition. The ropes were frayed, the sails old and patched, and the hull was leaking badly, but our cargo was light, and we rode high in the water, making good time under a strong wind.

Nine days out, the wind had risen to a gale, but even our rapid speed toward home did not interest me. I went to bed that night thoroughly bored—so bored, in fact, that I started reading some of the captain's Christian books. One of them set me to thinking: *What if these things are true? What if there is a God?* With a shudder, I slammed the book closed. If there was a God, I had been shaking my fist in His face and was in grave danger.

I was awakened by a spray of water in my face. The ship was pitching and wind howled through the open hatch and down the steps. I swung out of my bunk ready to run up and curse the person who had left the hatch open, but the water was up to my knees. I found my boots, pulled them on, then waded to the ladder.

On my way up to the deck, I met the captain coming down. He ordered me back to get my knife. He needed everyone's help to cut loose the rigging. The top of one of the masts had broken off, and some of the spars, suspended by the rigging, were swinging around the deck like battering rams.

Another man went up the ladder before me and was immediately washed overboard into the sea by a huge wave.

I have seen some bad storms at sea, but this one was by far the worse. Its force was so severe that it had torn away the upper timbers on one side of the ship, and the ship was beginning to sink. We jammed our bedding and clothes into the holes and cracks in the side. Over these we nailed boards, but still the sea gushed in.

All that day, we could do no more than man the pumps and operate a bucket brigade. I pumped hard—as did everyone else, because it was that or die—but the storm went on and on, exhausting us to the point of collapse. The wind was blowing so hard that it seemed to suck the breath right out of my lungs, and the driving rain stung any exposed skin like someone was throwing gravel at me.

We pumped until we could hardly stand up. Then we exchanged with someone on the bucket brigade

and bailed water until our backs nearly broke. And still, we were barely keeping up with the leaks.

The wind and freezing rain were vicious, and we—who had been in hot, tropical climates—were chilled to the bone even though we were working so hard. My old tropical fever seemed to return. I shivered and sweated at the same time and became so weak that my legs began to buckle beneath me.

When I could no longer work the pump, the captain ordered me to take the wheel and steer the ship. "Tie yourself to the helm with a rope!" he shouted. "That way you won't be washed into the sea."

Without realizing what I was saying, I shouted back, "If this be it, the Lord have mercy on us!" A few minutes later while I stared into the stinging rain, my words came back to my mind and I wondered, *Why would the Lord—if there is one—have mercy on someone like me who makes jokes denying His existence and daring Him to strike me dead?*

For the first time, I became really frightened—not just that I was about to die in this storm, but that after death I might have to face God. As the storm raged on, I tried to remember my religious training as a child. Would God forgive me? I didn't know, but I remembered a scary passage from the Book of Proverbs about fools who refuse God's correction. I had memorized it as a boy with my mother, and it said,

I also will laugh at your ~~calamity~~ disaster; I will mock when your fear cometh; When your fear cometh

as desolation, and your destruction cometh as a whirlwind; when distress and anguish cometh upon you. Then shall they call upon me, but I will not answer; they shall seek me early, but they shall not find me.

It seemed as if that was exactly what was happening to me, including the whirlwind. Did that mean that God would not answer me? That I wouldn't be able to find Him? That's what it felt like. Every time a wave broke over my head, the phrase went through my mind: "They shall seek me early, but they shall not find me."

"Oh, Lord!" I cried aloud. "Please let me find You!" No one could have heard me over the roar of the storm, but I wouldn't have cared. For the first time, I wanted God's mercy. And for the first time I began to see how I had rejected and scorned Him.

But as the wind and rain pulled at my body, another thought came to me: I, who had doubted God's very existence, was now acknowledging Him, even though it was in fear. And another verse my mother had taught me—again from Proverbs—came to me: "The fear of the Lord is the beginning of wisdom." Something was happening to me. The Lord was answering my prayer, at least to the point that I began to believe that He existed. Maybe there was still hope of my finding Him.

As the hours passed, the storm slowly subsided, and at about six that evening, word was passed that the pumping had lowered the water in the ship to a safe level. If no more damage was done, the ship might remain afloat.

I was finally given a break and fell into my bunk for a much needed rest, but we were not yet out of danger. The ship was still a wreck. Another storm would sink her. The pigs and sheep and chickens that we used for food had been washed overboard, and most of our food had been soaked and ruined. All we had left was a barrel of salted codfish and some hog food.

In the following days we made slow progress, having had most of our sails blown away, and I took my turn at the pump to keep us from sinking. But when I was off duty, I borrowed a Bible and read it. And when I was on duty, I reviewed what I had read, seeking God all the while.

I prayed a prayer of repentance, thanking God for saving us from the storm and asking God to forgive me for my evil ways. Slowly a calm confidence replaced my fear. I received an amazing grace, a faith that God had forgiven me and had saved my soul as He had so often saved my body.

Finally, five days after the storm, early one morning before the sun rose, the sailor on watch yelled out, "Land ho!" We all gathered on deck, and sure enough, off on the eastern horizon there appeared what seemed to be a mountainous coast ending in three islands—exactly what we expected to see as the northwest coast of Ireland.

We had a feast to celebrate, eating most of our remaining food and cheering one another up at our good fortune. And then the sun came up. What had looked like a coastline turned into a fog bank that evaporated as the morning progressed.

The next morning a storm blew up from the wrong direction, and we were blown far off course. Because of the fragile nature of our damaged ship, we could not fight the storm and had to go where it took us until it blew itself out and the wind again changed to a favorable direction.

After that, days turned into depressing weeks as we crept east. And in that cold north sea, without much food and working many hours a day at the pumps with no warm clothes, we were wasting away.

When one man finally died of starvation, the sailors—always a superstitious lot—began to think that something or someone was causing all of their trouble. Because they had heard me boldly challeng God to destroy me, even the captain suggested that I might be the "Jonah" who was bringing them bad luck. "Maybe we ought to throw him overboard," the men began to mutter.

I frankly don't know what kept them from doing so. It must have been God again.

Finally, four weeks after the storm damaged the ship, we drifted within true sight of the coast of Ireland and slowly made our way into the protected harbor of Lough Swilly.

Two hours after we dropped anchor, the wind's direction changed again and blew so violently that had we still been at sea, the ship most certainly would have sunk.

Chapter 11

The Slave Trader

Hamilton interrupted Newton and said, "Wait a minute. I don't understand. If this was when you repented and became a Christian, when were you a slave trader? You haven't told me about your being a slave trader yet."

Newton looked uncomfortable. "I'm ashamed to say that I became captain of a slave ship *after* my conversion."

"What?" asked the astounded boy. "You mean to say that even though you repented of other sins, of . . . of cursing God and behaving like a selfish pig— you mean to say that you thought nothing of enslaving other human beings?"

"That is the sorry truth," admitted Newton.

"But why?"

"As the prophet Jeremiah once said, 'The heart is deceitful above all things, and desperately wicked: who can know it?' For that reason, we easily fool ourselves into accepting the world's standards rather than God's standards of right and wrong."

Newton stood up and went to the window, looking out into the quiet night. "So-called 'good people' may disapprove of someone who treats a slave poorly," he went on, "but our whole society—with the exception of a few of us abolitionists—accepts slavery itself as 'the natural order.' People see it just as the way things are, neither good or bad in itself."

"Not black people," Hamilton said bitterly. "We know how evil slavery is, and we would never keep slaves or sell someone into slavery."

Newton turned back from the window. "Ah, but that's not necessarily true," he said. "Slavery is very common in Africa. In the various tribes and villages, anyone who is rich or powerful enough will have slaves, usually taken as captives in intertribal warfare."

Hamilton shifted uncomfortably. "Yeah, but that's different. Getting captured and taken to a neighboring village isn't so bad. There's always the possibility of escape or rescue. My people would never take someone away from their native country, their own people, and their familiar ways all the way across the ocean to make them work in some foreigner's fields."

"I agree. Being snatched from your homeland, having families ripped apart and shipped overseas is a terrible thing, worse than being a slave in your own country. But how do you think most slave traders get their slaves? Occasionally, European traders kidnap unwary natives and carry them off into captivity, but in most cases they buy them from African chiefs and tribal leaders. That's what Clow was doing when he went upriver to trade. That's what I was doing before I got on board the *Greyhound* to go back to England."

Hamilton looked sullenly down at the floor. The idea that the leaders of his own people were involved in slavery was hard to swallow.

"I should acknowledge," continued Newton, "that some of those tribal wars were engineered or at least encouraged by the slave traders. But my point is this, when society calls something right that is really wrong, then it takes time for God to reeducate His children. Long ago, much of society—even godly people—accepted polygamy where one man had more than one wife. It took time for God to teach His people otherwise. Through God's Word, the Bible, the Holy Spirit convicts us of sin. Then, if we are not too stubborn and bullheaded, God can help us change."

Newton turned back to the window. "Maybe someday everyone will realize that slavery is wrong, but that's not the way it is now. It takes time." His voice drifted off, as if he were not really talking to Hamilton.

The boy did not like what he was hearing very much, but he could see some truth in it. Abruptly he said, "So what about my mother? When did you take her from Africa?"

For a few minutes Newton didn't answer. Just as Hamilton was about to ask again, the man turned and came back to his chair. "That was not for some time yet," he said, continuing his story.

✧ ✧ ✧ ✧

Back in England, it was obvious to everyone who knew me that I had changed greatly. Many thought that I had just grown up, that my time in Africa had made a man of me, but I was ready to tell anyone who asked that it was God. God had changed my heart and not so long ago either.

One person who noticed the change in my character was a wealthy businessman who owned several ships. He was actually the friend that my father had gone to to seek help in obtaining my release from Clow.

In 1749 he offered me the position of first mate on the *Brownlow*. I accepted and was grateful that I had plenty of time before sailing to visit Mary. I wanted to ask her to marry me, and even obtained her parents' permission, but I waited until the last moment.

We were walking in her rose garden in Kent. Everything was perfect, so I said, "Mary, I want to ask you something very important."

She looked at me with her sparkling eyes and smiled in that disarming way she has, and suddenly I lost my courage. *Why would a beautiful girl like this want to marry me*, I thought. I stuttered and stammered, but finally all I could manage was, "Would it be all right if I wrote you a letter?"

Mary nodded, and that gave me a little more courage, so I said, "Before I sailed on the *Harwich* I wrote you several times, but you did not answer me. Will you answer me this time?"

She blushed, and I wondered if it was because my last letter had mentioned my love for her, but she said, "I was embarrassed by my poor penmanship, but this time I'll answer your letter."

Unfortunately, that was the end of it. We said goodbye, and I left for Liverpool.

As soon as I left, I could have kicked myself for being such a coward, but I did write the letter and posted it when I was only a short distance from her home.

The days of waiting that followed were almost unbearable. Finally, her answer came just before we were to sail. I was so excited that at first I couldn't open the letter. When I did, I realized she had not rejected my gestures of love. In fact, she said that she didn't care for anyone else and would *probably* be willing to marry me upon my return.

That's all I needed to hear.

While on the voyage, I used all my free time to study the Bible and dream about Mary. Sometimes that helped the time go quickly, and sometimes it

seemed as though we would never get back.

When I finally returned to England, Mary and I did get married, but it was not long before Joseph Manesty wanted me to take out another of his ships, this time as its captain.

The *Duke of Argyle* sailed on August 11, 1750, with a crew of thirty. I was its captain, but not a very proud captain when we returned a year later with only fourteen of the original crew members. It was an unseaworthy old tub, and that seemed to make everything worse. There was mutiny, tropical fever, and much death on the Middle Passage—that stretch of ocean from Africa to America.

✧ ✧ ✧ ✧

"Wait a minute," interrupted Hamilton. "You say that you lost half your crew, but how many slaves died?"

"On many ships as many as one third of the slaves died on the Middle Passage."

"But how about on your ship?"

"I lost six."

"Out of how many?"

"About two hundred."

"So on this one voyage you were responsible for the death of six African people, and still you called yourself a Christian? I ought to shoot you right now," said Hamilton, gritting his teeth. He got up and paced around the room, stopping by Newton's chair as he waved his pistol at him.

"As I said before," said Newton calmly, "I am indeed worthy of death. All of us must die sometime, and if God has set this as my time, then so be it."

"Ha!" said Hamilton, throwing his hands into the air. "Would that bring the dead slaves back to life or free those who sweat in the cotton fields today?"

"It would not. And that is a very good point. You should think about what you really hope to accomplish by shooting me."

Hamilton felt the anger surging again. "What I'm trying to do is none of your business!" he snapped.

"I'm in charge here, and you are the guilty one." After all, he had the pistol, didn't he? After a few moments, the boy flopped down into his chair, breathing hard. "What happened on your other voyages?"

"On my last voyage, I lost no one, not a crew member or a slave."

"Oh, am I supposed to admire you for carrying everyone *safely* to slavery?"

"No. You asked. It was just a matter of information."

"What about the voyage that brought my mother over? Tell me about that!"

Chapter 12

Revolt at Sea

J ohn Newton wrinkled his brow as he recalled his slave-trading days. "The *Duke of Argyle* was so unseaworthy," he said, "that Joseph Manesty provided me with a new ship for my next voyage. This was the *African*, and I was its first captain. That was 1752."

"Did you say 1752? That's when my mother was taken across on the *African*," said Hamilton eagerly. "Did you know her?"

Newton shook his head. "I'm sorry. We seldom learned the names of any slaves. Was there anything . . . unusual about how your

mother looked or what she did? Something I might remember?"

"She was young—younger than I am now."

"I took very few children. I think God was starting to touch my conscience about the evil of slavery, and my first response was to try to clean up my involvement."

Newton paused and rubbed his chin with his hand as if searching his memory. "I gave an order to my crew that no slave should be mistreated on my ship, and I even put one crew member in irons for striking a slave woman unnecessarily."

Newton held up first one finger and then another as he counted the "reforms" he had made. "I refused to buy slaves who were not in good health. I took no sick, feeble, elderly, or any children under four feet tall. So your mother was probably among the youngest.

"I carried fewer slaves than the ship could hold so that there was more room below deck. Each day—when the weather permitted—they were brought up on deck for fresh air, and the holds were washed out.

"On Sundays I held church services for the slaves—though very few understood a thing—and prayed for their souls each night."

John Newton looked directly at Hamilton and their eyes locked. The muscles in the boy's face twitched and his eyes narrowed. As if reading Hamilton's mind, Newton threw his hands up in despair. "I know! You can't turn evil into good simply by cleaning it up a little. Evil is evil, and the only solution is to stop it."

To Hamilton's surprise, tears slid down Newton's face. Then the man sighed, closed his eyes, and continued his story.

✧ ✧ ✧ ✧

Things didn't go well on the *African*. To begin with, before we sailed I met Job Lewis, the midshipman who had tried to befriend me in the navy when I was on the H.M.S. *Harwich*. By then Lewis was a captain, but the owner of his ship had gone bankrupt, so I convinced Joseph Manesty to hire him to go with me on the *African*. But shortly after we arrived in Africa, Job became ill with fever and within eight days died.

Then I discovered that two of the crew were stealing the ship's stores of ale and selling it for their own profit on shore. They nearly got away with this by refilling the ships barrels with water, making them appear full. I had both men flogged—one with eleven lashes and the other with nineteen—and put them off the ship.

A few days later, I found the ship's carpenter trying to inspire a mutiny. I would have put him in irons and turned him over to the first man-o'-war for trial, but I couldn't afford to lose his services, so I gave him two dozen lashes and kept him on.

A week later, when we were offshore of one of the larger African towns, two crew members deserted ship and stole one of the ship's boats.

We had an unusual amount of fever among the crew, and I was concerned that I wouldn't have enough men to sail the ship as well as watch over the slaves. Without enough crew members, there was always the risk that the slaves might try to revolt. Though once at sea and with no experience sailing, the chances of them getting safely to land was very small.

But before any kind of a revolt could happen, three crew members attempted to inspire a mutiny among the crew. Their idea was that they would take over the ship, sail with its load of slaves to America, and pocket all the profits.

But they were a bumbling lot, and I found out about the plot before they did any damage. I put two of the mutineers in irons. The third one was so sick that he died a few days later.

Finally, we had a full load of slaves—207, as I recall—and set out on the Middle Passage. But I was dreadfully shorthanded with only twenty crew members.

Many of the slaves were terrified when we sailed out of sight of land. Their only experience had been traveling by small canoes on rivers, and sailing for days on the sea drove some of them mad with terror. One afternoon while they were up on deck getting fresh air, I noticed one man looking back toward Africa. He staggered, obviously sick, as he walked around. Then, suddenly, he ran toward the side and dove into the sea.

We brought the ship about, lowered a boat, and

rescued him before he drowned, but before the night was over, he died from his fever and exposure.

It upset me that a person would dive into the sea rather than be carried into slavery. I blamed his behavior on his fever, thinking he was out of his mind. But then I remembered my days of slavery under Clow and Pea Eye. Maybe he wasn't so crazy. Maybe he suspected the horrors of the life ahead of him and preferred death.

To salve my conscience, I decided the next day to inspect the ship's hold myself to make sure the conditions of the slaves were bearable.

What I found were two men free from their irons and working with a chisel and a rock to free others. I immediately sounded the alarm, and after an inspection, we found several knives and handmade clubs.

With only twenty crewmen, and some of those still sick, it is quite possible that the slaves could have overpowered us if many more had gotten free. I was just in time.

✧ ✧ ✧ ✧

"No you weren't!" shouted Hamilton as he jumped to his feet. "You came too soon. They would have been free. Free! Don't you understand? FREE!"

Newton looked startled at the outburst. "Yes, well, maybe so. But we were in the middle of the Atlantic Ocean, and these slaves were not seamen. They would have had no idea how to sail a ship, or navigate to land. If they had overpowered and killed

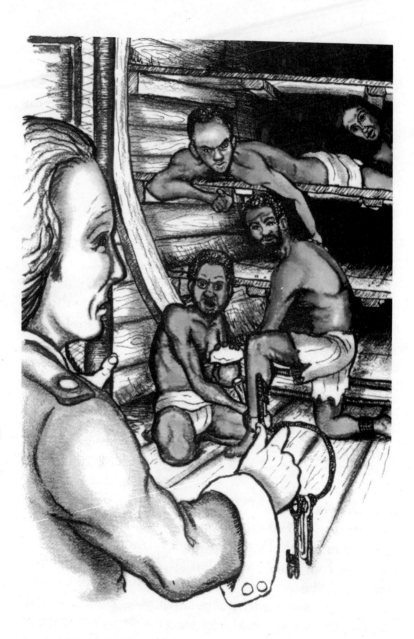

us, they, too, would have died drifting around at sea."

Hamilton slumped in his chair. After a few moments of silence, he said, "That was my mother, you know." His voice was subdued. "She told me about that attempt to revolt."

"Your mother? What was your mother?"

"You never found out, did you?"

"What are you talking about? What didn't I find out?"

"It was my mother who found that chisel up on deck and smuggled it back to the hold."

"Your mother did that? I . . . I thought it was one of the boys. I never put the women or the children in irons, you know. And there were four boys on board—about your age. I thought they supplied the tools."

"Nope," said Hamilton proudly. "My mama did it, and she got the first man free, too."

Suddenly, Newton began to weep. Soundless sobs at first that shook his whole body, and then he broke into great wails that seemed to go on and on.

Hamilton turned and looked out the window. He had heard men cry out before when they felt the whip of the overseer, but this mournful sobbing was different. He felt embarrassed, as though witnessing something too private to watch.

Finally, he grew impatient. "What are you crying for, man? You haven't been hurt."

Newton worked hard to stop the sobs and get himself under control. In a few minutes he wiped his face with his handkerchief and said, "No one has hurt me except myself. It's just what I did to those boys."

"The boys?" asked Hamilton. "What did you do to them?"

"I thought I needed a full confession from them. I didn't want another revolt, so I tried to find out who was responsible. It was obvious that certain of the men were involved, and I thought the boys got the tools. But they never confessed. I . . . I even used the thumb screws on them—not very hard—but . . . anyway, they never betrayed your mother, even under such pain."

Hamilton's face looked stricken. "What would you have done to my mother if you had found out that she was responsible?"

"I don't know." Newton blew his nose. "Probably I would have put her in irons. I wouldn't have needed to do anything more. The real danger came from the men, and the next day when we came upon another ship, I transferred fourteen men to it. It wasn't a slave ship, but when I explained to the captain that these men were the ringleaders of a slave revolt, he agreed to take them because he had plenty of room. I didn't send the boys over because I didn't think they would cause any more trouble, so—had I known your mother was involved, I wouldn't have sent her, either."

Hamilton stared blankly into the coals of the fire. He had found the man who had carried his mother into slavery. He had heard the whole story and now could take his revenge. He felt the pistol in his hands. It was several hours past midnight, and no one would hear the muffled sound of a pistol shot inside the house. If he was going to do it, this was the time.

Chapter 13

Amazing Grace

But there was one final question Hamilton wanted answered. "So when did you stop slave trading?"

"We sold the slaves in St. Christopher—one of the Caribbean Islands." Newton looked at the boy, recalling that Hamilton Jones said he and his mother were slaves in one of the American colonies. "Did your mother ever tell you how she got from there all the way to South Carolina?"

"Slaves don't choose where to live or when to move," said Hamilton sarcastically. "My mama got sold—twice, as I remember it.

133

The last person to buy her was Benjamin T. Bowdoin, and he was from South Carolina."

"I see."

Hamilton stuck out his jaw. "So? When did you stop slave trading?"

✧ ✧ ✧ ✧

I made one more voyage with the *African*. God must have been working on my heart because I took increasingly good care of the slaves. That was the trip where no one died, not a slave or a crew member, and such an achievement made me rather famous in Liverpool.

During the Middle Passage, however, I had a bout of fever from which I didn't think I would recover. I was out of my mind for several days, and the ship's doctor thought I was going to die. But I recovered and—though weak—felt like my old self by the time we landed in the Caribbean.

On the trip back to England, we ran into a bad storm, and the *African* barely survived. The ship, though relatively new, had never sailed very well, and when I complained about this to Joseph Manesty in Liverpool, he promised me a new ship he was having built—*The Bee*.

It was months before it would be finished, and so I enjoyed my time ashore with Mary. But every time I thought of going on another slave run, I was filled with dread. At the time, I didn't know if it was the sea, my growing dislike for slavery, or having to leave Mary, but I could hardly face the voyage. Then, two days before I was to go to sea, Mary and I were drinking tea in our parlor when I passed out and went crashing to the floor.

The doctor came and worked with me for over an hour before I regained consciousness and seemed to recover. But I had a severe headache, light-headedness, and blurred vision. Finally, the doctor decided that I was suffering the results of my recurring African fever and warned me never to go to tropical climates again.

What the doctor declared as a warning, I welcomed with relief. As soon as he said it, I felt better and realized how much I had dreaded the trip. Still, it was some time before I understood that my true distress was over slavery itself, and my heart and body were protesting what my mind had not yet understood.

But it was also another chapter in God's mercy to me. Later I heard that when *The Bee* was nearly loaded with slaves off the east coast of Africa, the slaves revolted—successfully this time—and killed the captain, the second mate, the doctor, and most of the crew. The wind drove the ship to shore and wrecked it. Most of the slaves escaped unharmed.

Again, had it not been for God's amazing grace to me, I would have been killed, too.

✧ ✧ ✧ ✧

"It sounds as if you never really *decided* on your

own to quit the slave trade," Hamilton said tartly. The growing confusion he'd been feeling lifted. He still had some justification for killing this man.

"I am embarrassed to say that—at the time—I stopped because I was too ill to go to sea. That's what stopped me. But since then, I have thought a lot about that amazing grace that God showed me throughout my life. If He cared for me when I rejected Him so often, then the least I can do is care for all the people for whom He sent His Son to die. The great grace God extended to me should be my attitude toward all people. I've been working on a little song that says what I mean." Then in a thin but clear voice, John Newton began to sing.

Amazing grace! how sweet the sound
  That saved a wretch like me!
I once was lost but now am found,
  Was blind but now I see.

The sweet melody seemed to hang in the stillness of the library as a faint, early morning light came in the window.

"That's me," said the former sea captain. "God saved my life over and over again until the hour I first believed. It's now my sole purpose to share that amazing grace with others."

"So that's why you are a preacher?"

"Yes."

"What makes you think that helps? Slave ships are still crossing the oceans."

"I believe it's a beginning. But there is much more to do . . . though maybe it now falls to someone else to do, since it appears"—Newton gestured toward the pistol in Hamilton's hand—"you are calling me to pay for my sins."

"What do you mean?" Hamilton said uncertainly.

"You said you came here to shoot me, didn't you?"

"Well . . . yes."

"Then my story is done, and I hope I have answered your questions."

Hamilton slowly raised the pistol. His mind raced with Newton's amazing story. Then the gun barrel began to waver. Hamilton made an effort to steady his aim as he thought, *This is what I came for, isn't it—to force this man to face his wickedness and make him pay for it? But . . . why isn't he afraid?*

As if reading his thoughts, Newton said, "I'm not afraid to die. God has forgiven my sins, but He does not always save us from the earthly consequences of our sins. Maybe that is what I must do"—he glanced out the window—"this morning. All I can say to you is that I am sorry, more sorry than I can ever express, though I preach against the evils of slavery whenever I get the chance."

The force of Newton's statement stunned Hamilton. Not once had the former slave trader made any excuses for what he had done. He had not tried to justify himself. The man knew he deserved to die for the havoc he had wreaked. Hamilton realized that this was the first white man he had ever known who understood how terrible the sin of slavery was.

In that moment, Hamilton realized that the man sitting calmly before him had truly repented—and had changed. And what was the last thing Newton said? That now he was preaching against the slave trade! *If I kill him*, thought Hamilton, *an earnest voice against slavery will be silenced, and African people everywhere will lose a true friend.*

Slowly, Hamilton stood up and placed the pistol inside his bag. "Once again," he said softly, "you have been given amazing grace. Maybe I need to find some for myself." Then the runaway slave boy turned and walked out of the vicarage into the sunrise.

More About John Newton

While there is no historical record of a slave or the son or daughter of a slave confronting John Newton about his role in the slave trade, he nevertheless became increasingly vocal against slavery. He joined abolitionist groups intent on outlawing the slave trade.

In 1785 Newton began helping William Wilberforce in his fight against slavery. Wilberforce, then a member of the British House of Commons, became the abolitionist movement's chief spokesperson.

In 1807, just months before John Newton died, Wilberforce secured enactment of legislation prohibiting the slave trade. Wilberforce then began the struggle for the complete abolition of slavery and, in 1823, was a founder of the Anti-Slavery Society. Ill health forced his retirement from Parliament in 1825. The Emancipation Bill abolishing slavery in England became law one month after his death.

John Newton wrote many well-known hymns, such as "Glorious Things of Thee Are Spoken" and "How Sweet the Name of Jesus Sounds." But no hymn is more widely known and loved than Newton's own testimony, "Amazing Grace."

Amazing grace! how sweet the sound
*   That saved a wretch like me!*
I once was lost but now am found,
*   Was blind but now I see.*

'Twas grace that taught my heart to fear,
*   And grace my fears relieved;*
How precious did that grace appear
*   The hour I first believed!*

Through many dangers, toils and snares
*   I have already come;*
'Tis grace has brought me safe thus far,
*   And grace will lead me home.*

The Lord has promised good to me,
*   His word my hope secures;*
He will my shield and portion be,
*   As long as life endures.*

Yes, when this flesh and heart shall fail
*   And mortal life shall cease;*

I shall possess, within the vail,
   A life of joy and peace.

The earth shall soon dissolve like snow,
   The sun forbear to shine;
But God, who called me here below,
   Will be forever mine.

by John Newton,
about 1776

For Further Reading

Bohrer, Dick, *John Newton: Letters of a Slave Trader* paraphrased by Dick Bohrer (Chicago: Moody Press, 1983).

Demaray, Donald E., *Amazing Grace!* (Winona Lake, Ind.: Light and Life Press, 1958).

Martin, Bernard, *John Newton: A Biography* (London: William Heinemann, Ltd., 1950).

Newton, John, *John Newton: Letters of a Slave Trader Freed by God's Grace* (Chicago: Moody Press, first published in 1764).

Swift, Catherine, *John Newton* (Minneapolis, Minn.: Bethany House Publishers, 1991).